A Touch in the Dark

Dr. Cassundra White-Elliott

This book is a work of fiction and was created from the author's imagination. However, there are a few factual incidents imbedded within that came directly from the author's life.

Published by CLF PUBLISHING, LLC. 3281 E. Guasti Road, Seventh Floor, Ontario, CA 91761.
(760) 669-8149.

Cover Design by Senir Design. Contact information- info@senirdesign.com.

Special thank you to cover model- Kierra N. (Williams) Benson.

ISBN 978-0-9899408-7-0

Printed in the United States of America.

Dedications

For all abuse victims.

May you walk in healing and deliverance.

Dr. C. White-Elliott

Acknowledgements

I acknowledge those who lovingly assisted with this project:

Merilyn Jolly

and

Kierra N. Benson

Thank you. Your assistance was invaluable, and you are greatly appreciated.

Preface

A Touch in the Dark was written to serve several purposes. Before delving into the various purposes of the novel, allow me to explain the meaning of the title and the front cover image.

The woman on the cover is dressed in a white gown to demonstrate purity and innocence. Her face is not shown purposefully in order to demonstrate her representation of all girls and all women. This woman, like many others throughout our land and foreign lands as well, has suffered abuse. As a result, she seeks healing and deliverance from the pain she has suffered and the residual scars she bears.

Black was chosen for the background color to show the contrast of the white gown (purity) and the pain in which she is enveloped.

The title- *A Touch in the Dark* -has a two-fold meaning. First, the touch the woman received as a child and/or as a teenager was a forbidden touch, a touch she should have never received from a person (or persons) with a perverted mind. That touch effects the touch she receives as an adult from the man she loves, namely her husband. The tainted touch she received in the past effects the innocence of the touch she receives today.

Although this book has several functions: to entertain, to encourage, to evoke questions and emotions, to cause one to wonder, and instill desire, it has a single primary purpose. The formal purpose of this book is to render healing or to at least demonstrate to those who are hurting that they can receive their own healing from past scars and walk in the victory of deliverance.

If you carry the scars of your past, prepare to release those scars as you read the book. Like the main character, you can be free. You can walk in healing as you are delivered from the terror and torment of past hurts.

If you are not the one who has suffered abuse, share this book with someone you know who has. Although the story itself is fictional, all accounts of abuse shared within are real. They were all experienced by the author herself. Just as the experiences are real, so is healing and deliverance.

Claim your freedom today!

I

After the lengthy flight from Los Angeles and dealing with the new airport security regulations and customs, Teri and Reggie were happy to finally arrive to their vacation destination. Not even taking a minute to unpack their suitcases, they quickly found a comfortable outfit, immediately changed their clothes, and went out to enjoy the evening breeze and sunset.

Teri opted to sit out on the veranda and enjoy the cool breeze, as she watched the other tourists saunter by. Couples were enjoying one another's company, and the children were laughing and playing. Her husband Reggie walked up quietly behind her, knelt down, and gently kissed her behind her ear as he handed her a glass of wine. Although she knew they were completely alone, his unexpected touch caused her body to stiffen. When he moved from behind her to sit in his chair on the other side of the small table, he looked directly into her eyes to get a sense of what she was feeling. Knowing he was watching her intently, she managed to smile, masking her true thoughts and emotions.

"How's my baby?" Reggie asked.

"All is well. This scenery is breathtaking," she replied as she lifted her eyes toward the sandy beach that was just steps away from their resort room door.

"So, are you enjoying our vacation so far?"

"Yes, for the thirty minutes that we have been here. Absolutely. How about you?" Teri asked her husband with sincere concern, although she knew he wasn't hard to please.

"Babe, I couldn't have asked for anything better. You did a great job of choosing this place. I like what I see so far."

Reggie and Teri have been married for nearly eight years. Every year, they make it a point to vacation in a brand new location, one they can explore together. This year, the vacation spot was a beautiful all-inclusive resort in Cancun.

Reggie and Teri are inseparable. Usually, when you see one, you see the other, except for when they are at work. They are a fun-loving, easy-going couple. Although they are very different, they are very compatible.

"So, what do you want to do first?" Reggie asked his beautiful wife as he sipped his wine.

"I'm hungry. Those snacks they give on the plane only hold you for a brief moment. "

"Yeah, but you have to admit, they are much better than the peanuts and pretzels they used to give out."

"That's true," Teri said with a little laugh.

"What do you have a taste for?"

"Nothing in particular. Maybe seafood. What about you?"

"I have always said I wanted to try native ceviche."

"Sounds good," Teri agreed.

Upon arriving to the island, the guests were given a map of the resort and a list of all restaurants and amenities. Reggie retrieved the map and began to scout out the restaurants. He located the seafood restaurant on the opposite end of the beach. The couple slid their feet into their sandals and made their way to dinner.

As they walked upon the lighted path, they held hands and stopped several times along the way to take pictures of the scenery and each other.

Arriving at their destination, their mouths began to water with anticipation of the deliciously prepared food. Instead of sitting in the restaurant, they opted to find available lounge chairs on the beach. They relaxed with their dinner plates balanced on their laps and enjoyed the meal and each other's company.

Towards the end of the meal, Teri discovered *she* was dinner for several ants that were feasting on her feet. She jumped up from the pain the ant bites caused. There were tiny red bites all over her feet.

After dinner, the couple found a show to enjoy in the outside theatre. Finding seats was difficult because it seemed everyone at the resort wanted to watch the show. Luckily, a pair of teenagers changed their minds, and Reggie and Teri were able to slip quickly into their seats. The locals put on a performance that kept all the viewers laughing from beginning to end. When the show ended, Reggie escorted his wife back to their room. They were exhausted from a full day of traveling and the evening's festivities, plus their bellies were filled with ceviche, cream-filled churros, and margaritas.

Not really taking a lot of time to explore the room before dinner, Teri saw that the bathtub was actually a Jacuzzi made for two. It was nice and deep and had powerful jets. They looked at each other and immediately began to undress. They both were desperate to relax after a long week at work and an afternoon of travel.

As Reggie and Teri soaked, the warm water and jets helped to ease all the tension of the flight and the forty-five minute bumpy ride from the airport to the resort. By nightfall, the couple was totally relaxed, after having had a wonderful first day of their seven-day vacation.

Just before retiring to bed, Reggie rubbed ointment on Teri's feet where the ants had bitten her. She enjoyed every stroke of his fingers as he attended to her every need. As she watched him, she knew without a shadow of doubt he loved her unconditionally. But, that did not seem to cure the inner torment she sometimes faces.

As the night wore on, Teri enjoyed the comfort of her husband's strong arms. She loved to press her soft but firm body against his. He made her feel secure. She silently prayed that every night would be that peaceful.

For the entire vacation, Reggie and Teri explored the resort and various other parts of Cancun, ate good food, enjoyed wonderful weather and entertainment, and basked in each other's love.

Finally, the time came for them to depart. Although they weren't looking forward to bumping back to the airport on the streets of Cancun, going through international customs, or sitting in a row of three on the airplane, they were ready to head back to the States. No matter where they went on vacation, they always looked forward to returning to their own home of peace and solitude. Of course, they didn't have room service there and pre-prepared meals to enjoy, but as it is often said, 'There is no place like home.' So, they re-packed their suitcases and bid the resort and the staff goodbye.

On the trip home, Teri rested her head against the airplane's seat. She was thankful that the adventure through customs was nearly painless. It was nothing like it was leaving the United States or entering in. The NSA had everything so tight; she didn't think any criminals or terrorists could slip by as they had done in the past.

As she began to relax for the preparation of the take-off, she quickly reminisced about the seven days of vacation she and Reggie had just enjoyed. She reached over and took her husband's hand into her own. He smiled at her as he took out a book to read on the flight. He too had enjoyed himself immensely. For him, it was nothing like taking a break from the tedious technical work he did five and sometimes six days a week. His mind needed the mental rest while his body needed the physical rest. He had just finished another major project at work, so this vacation couldn't have come at a better time.

Shortly after the plane had lifted off and reached the proper elevation for the flight, Teri began to doze off. Every now and then, the plane would hit an air pocket, and she would awaken. Although her sleep was disturbed periodically, her disposition couldn't be. The trip to Cancun was one of the best vacations she had taken, and she was just savoring the moment. She was basking in the afterglow.

As she continued to reminisce, it suddenly hit her! She had not had any episodes during the trip. With that thought, a smile covered her face. All had gone well! No flashbacks! No weird feelings! Nothing!

All had gone well!

2

As soon as Reggie and Teri landed at LAX, Teri received an emergency page from Kaiser Permanente Hospital. "That's the hospital," she said as she lifted her pager up. Reggie nodded. He knew the procedures well by now. As Teri responded to the page, Reggie retrieved their luggage from the baggage claim.

Hauling Teri's extensive wardrobe along with his single suitcase, Reggie found his wife in the exact same spot he had left her in just minutes before. It was as if she was glued to her spot. He couldn't read the look on her face. It was one he had never seen before, but he knew enough to know that it wasn't good.

"What is it, babe?" he asked with concern, still trying to read her face.

"There was a drive-by shooting in East L.A. A two-year-old girl was caught in the crossfire and was shot in the head. The bullet is lodged in her brain. I have been requested to do the surgery," Teri said with tears streaming down her face. She felt so sorry for the little girl, even though she had not yet met her. Teri's heart went out to her and her family.

"Okay, let me get you to Kaiser," Reggie said, ready to move into action and get to their car.

"No, you don't need to do that. The hospital is sending a squad car here to the airport. I have already given them our terminal."

"They're sending the police?" Reggie asked in alarm.

"Yes, they are the only ones who can cut through traffic. Time is of the essence. We don't want to risk our safety trying to get there or even getting a ticket in the process."

"Oh, okay. Look, babe! I think they're here already. Wow, that was fast. Will you be okay to go through with this? You seem a little shaken up," Reggie asked as a squad car approached with flashing lights.

"I'll be fine. I'm just thinking about the patient," Teri answered quickly, as she kissed her husband goodbye and handed him her carry-on bag. As she walked out, the police officer called her name on the bullhorn, "Dr. Langston!" She grabbed her hospital ID, flashed it to him and quickly jumped into the squad car. She was immediately whisked away to the hospital.

On the drive over, the police officer was trying to make small talk. He asked her questions, such as how long she has been a doctor and whether or not she had operated on a drive-by victim before. With Teri's brief answers and silence, he finally stopped asking questions and focused on driving as he weaved in and out of traffic.

Before long, she was safely delivered to the hospital. She dropped off her purse and personal belongings in her office and went up to the surgical floor. She was ready to be prepped for surgery. An attendant was waiting for her with scrubs and a mask to place on her once she was properly sanitized. As she washed her hands, she noticed she was slightly trembling. So, she said a quick prayer.

Lord God, you are the great I Am. You are the only healer. Use me, Lord. I am your vessel. Please deliver this little girl safely through this procedure, in Jesus' name. Amen.

With clean, gloved hands, Teri was guided into the operating room. Standing at the head of the operating table, Teri was completely quiet. She failed to command the operating room, so the head nurse jumped to action.

"Dr. Langston is here. Is everyone ready?" the head attending nurse asked. Everyone nodded behind their masked faces. Teri continued to look intently at the little girl whose body was almost lifeless. The little girl was lying on her stomach in order to expose the back of her head. Her face was placed in a opening in the operating table to allow for breathing and to lock her head into a stationery position. She had been given a general anesthesia to relax her entire body, so she wasn't moving a muscle.

As Teri continued to survey the little girl, a tear unexpectedly sprang from one of her eyes. This surprised Teri. She had always prided herself on keeping her emotions out of the operating room. Sure, she felt for her patients and their well-being, but she never allowed herself to be emotional while operating. Her ability to concentrate and perform top-notch, pristine surgeries with A-1 stitching had caused her to gain great notoriety amongst brain surgeons. For this reason, she was requested for this particular surgery.

However, this situation was different. Never had she operated on someone this young due to a gunshot wound. Different or not, she was determined to have the same results: a successful surgery and a healthy patient.

"Are you ready, Doc?" the nurse asked. Teri nodded, retained her composure, and began the procedure. With expert hands, she slowly pushed the scalp tissue back that covered the area of the skull where the bullet had entered the back of the little girl's head. Afterward, she had to drill a larger opening in the cranium to get to the bullet that had sunken deeper into the brain tissue.

After several hours, the surgery was complete, with the bullet removal successful. The entire staff was fatigued, especially Teri as she had just gotten off a long flight. Thankfully, she had taken a nap during the flight, not knowing she would need her strength as soon as she touched ground.

Retiring to the doctors' lounge, Teri picked up the phone and dialed her husband's number. After three rings, Reggie answered while half asleep.

"Hey, sleeping beauty," Teri teased.

"Oh, hey babe. How did everything go?" Reggie asked, hearing the fatigue in his wife's voice.

"Well, I successfully removed the bullet. But, honey you should have seen her. She was so small," Teri said getting choked up again.

"I know, honey. But, she will be okay now; I'm sure. Are you ready to come home or is there more for you to do before you can leave?"

"The only thing that is left to do is to talk to her parents. I just wanted to change my clothes very quickly. I didn't want them to see all the blood. I'll call you back in a few. Just stay by the phone. I'm ready to pass out."

"Okay, babe. I'll be ready when you are. I'm going to get up and start getting redressed now." Reggie had gone home and made himself comfortable. Based on prior experiences, he knew his wife would be in surgery for several hours. So, he had taken the opportunity to get a little rest.

While Teri was sleeping on the plane, he had opted for a little silent reading. He was a great Tom Clancy fan, so he had picked up Clancy's latest novel for the trip. On the flight home, he was able to finish it. He knew once he returned to work on Monday, it was pretty much over for getting any reading in. When he came home from work each day, he was exhausted, and reading was the furthest thing from his mind.

At the hospital, Teri quickly changed her clothing, grabbed her white doctor's coat, and went to the waiting room located down the hall from the surgical room. She quickly looked for a Hispanic couple. There were so many people there; it was hard to see who was who. She quietly called out their names, "Mr. and Mrs. Chavez." From the midst of the group, the little girl's parents emerged.

"Si?" they both responded. Looking a little taken aback, Teri did not know exactly where to proceed, as she does not speak Spanish. Immediately, a teenage boy came over to translate for his parents.

"My mom and dad don't speak English. Is this about my sister?"

To verify she had the right family, Teri asked, "Jessica Chavez?" The boy quickly nodded. "And your name?"

"I'm Javier." Teri wanted to make a mental note of who she had shared information with. Sometimes patients or their parents will claim they didn't know a certain piece of information or that no one came to speak to them. Teri always kept a record of who she spoke with after each surgery.

Teri quickly filled Javier in on Jessica's surgery and her current prognosis. Javier relayed the information to his parents. They screamed and hugged each other as they cried. They were excited to hear the news of the surgery's success. Teri then politely walked out to give the family privacy.

After checking in on Jessica, to find her still resting under the influence of the anesthesia and the medicine that was being administered to usher her into a coma, Teri called Reggie to come pick her up. As hospital policy, she would return in three hours to check on her patient. Most doctors opted to sleep in the doctors' lounge while they waited the three hours instead of going home and coming back, but Teri not only wanted to take a short nap, but she also wanted to take a shower, and she preferred to do so in the privacy of her own bathroom.

3

A month later, before leaving the hospital for the day, Teri instructed Jessica's nurses to begin to wean her off the drugs that had induced her coma. The medically induced coma was necessary for the brain to heal or at least begin the healing process and allow it to reach a certain point. From the brain scans that were taken each week, Teri could see Jessica's cerebellum was healing well.

When Teri walked in the door of her home from her afternoon shift at the hospital, she was greeted with the pleasant aroma of Pasta Carbonara and garlic cheese bread. As she allowed her nose to lead her straight into the kitchen, she found her husband tossing a delicious-looking Caesar salad. They greeted each other with a smile and an air kiss. To assist, Teri walked to the wine refrigerator and removed a bottle of Stella Rosa II Conte d'Alba Rosso. She thought red wine went perfectly with Italian meals.

"How was your day, handsome?" she asked her husband as she opened the bottle to allow it to breathe before pouring it into the wine glasses.

"Interesting, to say the least. We received instructions for a new space shuttle, and I was chosen to be on the special team to construct the new prototype. We were told we are required to have it ready by next spring."

"Sounds exciting. Congratulations on being chosen. Sounds like you guys will be working around the clock for a while."

"Well, we will definitely need to work plenty of overtime to get everything accomplished in less than a year."

The two sat comfortably at the granite counter topped island that sits in the middle of their massive kitchen instead of going to the dining room. While eating the delicious dinner Reggie had prepared and enjoying the sweet wine, they finished their conversation, and Teri brought Reggie up to speed on Jessica's prognosis and her other patients.

After dinner, the couple retreated to the family room to relax with a good movie. While Reggie surfed the numerous channels, Teri turned her attention back to the dinner she had just consumed.

"Honey, where did you get that recipe for that pasta dish?" she questioned with a smile on her face, for she was sure she already knew the answer.

"From the..." Reggie started.

"Cooking Network," Teri finished with a laugh.

"Yeah, you know me. I try to pick up a new recipe here and there for your dining pleasure," Reggie said smiling as he stroked his wife's feet that were lying on his lap.

"Yeah, we know that is your all-time favorite station besides the SyFy channel."

"Oh, look who's talking. You watch HGTV all day on your days off. And, I see you have gathered many innovative ideas that are displayed throughout our home," Reggie said as he pointed to several updates Teri had made. They both had a good laugh from chiding one another about their favorite pastimes.

Finally finding a good movie to satisfy both their tastes, the couple settled in for a quiet and relaxing evening. As the night wore on, Teri moved over to her favorite relaxation spot: her Lazy Boy recliner. She leaned it back, and before long, she dozed off. All it took for her to relax was a good meal and one glass of wine.

Reggie loved to cook. He and his wife both worked full time, but at least his schedule was mainly nine to five, unless a special project needed to be completed. Teri, on the other hand, worked in the mornings, in the afternoons, in the evenings, and on call. She had to go when the patients needed her. That is the way the world of medicine works, especially for surgeons.

Reggie immediately grabbed a soft fleece throw to cover his wife when he heard her soft raspy snoring. As he placed the fleece down the length of Teri's body, his hand accidentally brushed against one of her breasts. Teri immediately awoke and sat straight up.

"Sorry, babe," Reggie responded, knowing his wife's sensitivity. He had tried to be careful, but he hadn't even realized his hand had touched her.

"Oh, it's okay," Teri said trying to reassure her husband that she was okay. She didn't want to alarm him or cause him to feel bad for a mere accident. She knew he wouldn't intentionally try to harm her.

As she turned on her side and pulled the fleece back up to her neck, Teri closed her eyes and pretended to go back to sleep. But, sleep was the furthest thing from her mind.

Over the years, Teri had become more and more sensitive about her breasts. She rarely liked for them to be touched, even in the slightest. And, she guarded them as if though her life depended on it. One would think that for the length of time she had been married, she would have become freer with her body and much more relaxed when she interacted with her husband. But, it was quite the opposite. At times, she felt free. While at other times she felt very reserved and cautious. She couldn't explain it, and she desperately wished things weren't the way they are, but the reality is- it is what it is.

As she lay there, her mind travelled back to when she was twelve or thirteen years old. It was summer time, and she did what she had done for all the past few summers: she went to her grandmother's house to spend the summer with her. Teri loved being in her grandmother's company and her grandmother always looked forward to Teri coming over. Teri loved spending time with her grandmother and learning the history of their family. She also loved going to church with her grandmother on Sundays and stopping by Golden Bird Fried Chicken on the way home.

During this particular summer visit, one of Teri's grandmother's neighbors asked if Teri could come over and do a little cleaning. Teri's grandmother, whom she called Granny, consented. The neighbor was an elderly heavyset man whom Granny called Dad. Dad lived alone with his ailing wife who was bedridden. Dad was tasked with cooking for himself and cleaning after himself, unless someone else made herself available to take those tasks on.

Teri had gone to Dad's home several times with Granny to clean, but she had never gone alone. Her familiarity with Dad made her comfortable, and she didn't mind going over there to do a little house work. Her mother and grandmother had her well versed in the art of cleaning. As a young teenager, she didn't do it as well as they did, but she definitely knew what needed to be done and how to do it. She even knew what materials to use and what cleansers what get the job done.

When she arrived, Dad asked her to wash the dishes and clean the kitchen, and he would give her a few dollars. She readily consented to his list of chores and got right to it without delay. There was a funny smell in Dad's home, and Teri did not want to belabor her time there. She wanted to do the chores and set herself free. The list of chores was light, and the fee he was willing to pay was light also. But not having expensive taste or a lavish lifestyle at twelve or thirteen, a few dollars was all Teri needed to go to the corner store to get her favorite snack: a bottle of Pepsi and a Snicker candy bar. That would cost her all of seventy-five cents. She would even have enough money to go back to the store the next day to get her snack all over again.

After Teri finished cleaning the kitchen, Dad placed her money on the counter. As she picked up the money and prepared to leave, Dad said, "I'll give you an extra quarter if you give me a hug." Teri thought his request was odd to say the least, especially with the added part about paying an extra quarter. Nevertheless, Teri leaned in to hug the old man and received the surprise of a lifetime. When she hugged Dad, he kissed her. He stuck his old fat tongue into her mouth and at the same time, he grabbed one of her small breasts and squeezed it. She gagged from the horrible taste of his tongue as she wondered why he would do such a foul thing, especially with his dying wife right in the next room.

Teri was completely grossed out by what she had just experienced. She choked back her tears, masked her horror and immediately left. She nearly ran back across the street to her grandmother's. She never told a soul about how she was humiliated for a quarter, but she definitely never forgot it.

That experience left a bad taste in Teri's spirit. From that incident and others to come, she learned men would pay for anything. Any and everything they could ever want had a price tag on it, and they believed they could pay for anything their hearts desired. She found that to be the sad truth.

As she continued her summer vacation with her loving grandmother, she was careful to stay clear of Dad's home. When she walked to the store, she made sure not to go on his side of the street. And, when her grandmother went over there to clean, she never went with her- ever again.

If there was anything Teri learned from the incident with Dad, it was to stay clear of pedophiles. And that is exactly what she did when she learned who was who.

4

Three months later

As an engineer who was part of the design team for *NASA*'s new shuttle prototype, Reggie and his counterparts had been putting in long hours discussing the proper materials to be used, the weight, the interior and exterior dimensions, etc. Although this project was awe inspiring to work on and the team was certainly honored to have been chosen from several hundred engineers at *NASA*, they were very intimidated. All team members had studied and had even personally surveyed previous shuttle designs, but none of them had worked on any of the previous shuttles.

Because the engineers had been chosen from several *NASA* locations across the country, many of them had only met one another for the first time at the beginning of the project. But, with the long hours they had spent together over the few months they had been collaborating, they had quickly learned each other's temperaments, personalities, strong suits, eating patterns, marital status, etc.

One weekend, instead of the out-of-town team members flying back home, *NASA* flew all spouses and families to Los Angeles. This enabled each team member time to work on that Saturday morning and attend the regional *NASA* presentation dinner that evening without neglecting their families.

Normally, the out-of-town team members flew home between 5-7pm on Friday evenings and returned to Los Angeles between 7-9am on Monday morning. The days and evenings were long Monday through Thursday before the engineers retired to their hotel rooms, but over the weekend, they refreshed their minds for a new start on Monday.

At the dinner banquet on Saturday, entire families attended to share in the presentations and the honors the engineers had bestowed upon them. Afterward, some of the couples who did not have young children decided to get out and explore the infamous city of angels. For many of them, it was their first time coming to the Golden State, and they were very much interested in touring Hollywood.

Reggie and Teri did not join the group that went out Saturday night, but Reggie did agree to be a driver for the Hollywood tour on Sunday. He and several of the other local team members pulled out their large SUV's and drove the out-of-towners through the local hot spots.

For lunch, the group went to Universal City Walk and had lunch at several different restaurants. Some had a taste for seafood, others had a taste for steak, and those with children opted for burgers and fries. Later that evening, each group met at the designated location at the designated time to make their way back to the hotel.

As Reggie and Teri sat in the front seat of their Cadillac Escalade, they patiently waited for their complete party to return.

So far, only Tim, Reggie's co-worker, and his wife Linda had returned.

Parked two cars over in a Lincoln Navigator sat another of Reggie's co-workers and her husband. They too were awaiting the arrival of two of the out-of-towners and their spouses. As Reggie, Tim, Teri, and Linda were making small talk, a loud disturbance was heard coming from the rear of the vehicle. Reggie and Teri quickly looked in the side-view mirrors to see what was transpiring.

Two of the out-of-town male team members were in each other's faces yelling back and forth. Not too far behind them, their wives were behaving the same way. The four of them were making a public spectacle of themselves, and it was quite embarrassing to the rest of the group. Hoping they would calm down on their own, everyone stayed put within the vehicles. No one could imagine what had happened to cause the couples to be in such an uproar. From the sound of things, it could become physical at any moment. Hopefully, that would not be the case.

To Reggie's knowledge, one couple was from New York, and the other was from Detroit. He wasn't aware that they knew one another. As a matter of fact, he was present when they first arrived and recalled them being introduced. They met and began making small talk. There was no indication that they had prior history.

After five minutes had passed and the yelling had only escalated, Reggie, Tim, and John, from the other vehicle, got out to try to diffuse the situation. At that point, after asking a few pointed questions, the finger pointing and accusations became clear.

Once the story had been told, it was learned Russell from New York and Stephanie from Detroit had gone to college together in Georgia and had apparently been romantically involved for several years until Russell left to join a branch of the armed services. Not long after his time in boot camp and being permanently stationed in another state, they lost contact because Stephanie graduated and moved to Detroit for a job. Now after basically being reunited after over a decade and a half, the sparks were flying between them as if they had just seen each other yesterday in college.

Instead of telling their spouses who the other person was, they pretended to have just met. But the chemistry between them was obvious to even a stranger passing by. Once the secret had been uncovered, it had not set well with their spouses.

The night before, several of the team members and their spouses had gone out for drinks and to dance. On the dance floor, Russell and Stephanie were dancing rather closely and seemed to be in a world of their own. This is when the speculations and questions first began. But things had not ended there.

When everyone retreated back to the hotel, Melissa, Russell's wife, woke up to find him missing in the middle of the night. Shortly afterward, he came walking back in with a bucket of ice saying he was thirsty and needed a cold drink. Not knowing how long he had been gone, Melissa dismissed it. In another room, Stephanie's husband Frank was sleeping very soundly and had not even known Stephanie had slipped out.

Now, at Universal City Walk another couple had come up to the two couples and had mistaken Russell and Stephanie to be married to one another rather than to their actual spouses because they had been seen at the hotel bar the night before sharing drinks and intimate conversation. This caused a lot of confusion between all four spouses and the speculations continued. Melissa and Frank began to put the pieces together and started asking even more questions. Neither of them wanted to be made a fool of, so they both were demanding answers.

With Reggie, Tim, and John acting as mediators, the truth was brought to the surface. Obviously, Russell and Stephanie's intentions were not honorable because it took a little while before they finally admitted they knew each other and had met for a drink late the night before.

When asked why that was such a big secret, both parties were hesitant to explain. The truth of the matter was Stephanie had only married Frank last year because she had become pregnant after dating him for a few months, and she wanted her child's father to be in the home. She had grown up in a broken home and had vowed to herself that if she ever had children, she would work extra hard to ensure her marriage would not be another statistic for the divorce rate. She didn't want her child to have to endure being shifted between two parents who lived in two different homes. Although she didn't love Frank the way she really wanted to love the man she was married to, she married him for the sake of her unborn child. She had hoped over time her feelings would deepen, but that had yet to happen.

Also, Russell and Melissa's marriage had been on the rocks for some time, and they had already been discussing a possible separation. Melissa had hoped this trip would be a step in the right direction for them to spend a little time together away from home and to get their marriage back on track. Little did all of them know what the weekend would truly bring.

Maybe seeing an old flame had Russell and Stephanie thinking about the possibilities for their futures and an opportunity where they could possibly be happy. Neither of them actually revealed anything about their marriage to the group, but their own personal thoughts and desires had driven them to see if the flame they had once shared was still burning.

Finally separating the two couples and getting them into separate vehicles, the entire group caravanned back to the hotel to drop the guests off and head to their respective homes. Some of the other couples were concerned about leaving Russell and Frank alone with one another, but they figured adults had to work out their own issues. Plus, not having a personal relationship with them because they were both from out of town, no one really knew how to approach them.

The drive from Universal City was quiet! No one said a word. It was an uncomfortable situation for everyone involved and for those who witnessed it. All undoubtedly were thinking about their own marriage and the strength of the bond they have with their spouse. They couldn't help but to. Anytime people witness a situation occurring in life, they have a tendency to think about what they would do or how they would feel if that same situation happened to them. Those who were single were probably being very thankful at that moment.

Only a fly on the wall could tell what conversations took place in the homes of the locals and in the hotel rooms of the guests later that night. Some may have prayed for the two couples, others may have made smart comments or cracked jokes at their expense, and some may have said nothing at all and were just thankful that it wasn't them.

When Teri and Reggie returned home, they immediately went upstairs to get undressed and prepare for bed. They were physically and emotionally drained from a full week of work, the banquet on Saturday evening, and a full day out on Sunday. Witnessing someone else's marital drama and intervening to keep people from getting hurt was emotionally draining.

"So," Teri began, "did you have any idea any of that was going on?"

"No, but I did see Russ and Stephanie speaking from time to time, but I didn't suspect anything. I didn't even give it a second thought."

"I guess you never know what people are going through or dealing with that drives them to get involved with another person. I'm not saying Russ and Steph are involved with each other. They only just saw each other again yesterday after what-fifteen years."

"As far as we know. Remember, we don't know the whole story. For all we know, they could have met up anywhere before they came here."

"You know that's true. But, I don't want to speculate. I just hope they get their lives together because I am sure Frank and Melissa want some answers as to what their spouse's intentions are."

"Yeah, who wouldn't? I know if someone was making a move on you, I wouldn't sit idly by and let him have his way with you."

"Oh, you wouldn't, would you?" Teri said with a smile. She loved the attention her husband gave her when he was acting like a jealous husband. He wasn't the jealous type, but he certainly wasn't the weak type either. He knew where he stood with his wife, but he wasn't going to give another man any room to come in and take over either.

"Of course not. Any man that tries to come knocking on your door will need to get past me first."

"Yeah, I know you wrote "Taken" on my forehead, in that ink that only men can read," Teri said laughing.

"You're right. I did. I wrote it on our wedding night after you had gone to sleep." With a deep look of love in his eyes, Reggie pulled his wife over to him and said, "Come here. Let me look at you. With the long hours I've been working, we haven't seen much of each other."

"Yes, I know. Let's discuss it in the shower," Teri said with a sexy look in her eyes, as she pulled her husband over to the bathroom door and began to unbutton his shirt.

5

Six months after Jessica Chavez was released from the hospital, she was still required to attend physical therapy three times a week. Her therapist and parents weren't seeing much progress in the movement of Jessica's legs. Everything else was back on track: her speech, hand-eye coordination and the ability to feed herself. However, Jessica, who is now three years old, could not walk.

Prior to the accident, at two and a half years old, Jessica had been walking for a year and a half. After the accident eight months ago, she had not walked since. That was very devastating to her family, especially her parents.

After Teri stopped by to see Jessica at her physical therapy appointment, she passed Jessica's parents as she was getting onto the elevator to go to another appointment. She attempted to wave hello to them, but they completely ignored her. It was almost as though they pretended not to see her, but it was obvious to Teri that they did. She couldn't figure out why they were giving her the cold shoulder. But, at the moment, she couldn't spare time thinking about it. She was on her way to another appointment that she was actually about to be late for.

Getting off the elevator at the fifth floor, Teri was on her way to see her OB/GYN. She had been feeling unexplainably queasy for the last couple of weeks, and her menstrual cycle had not come as scheduled. When she arrived to the doctor's office, the nurse on duty greeted her warmly.

"Good afternoon, Dr. Langston. What brings you in today?"

"Hi, Sheila. I have a 12:15 appointment with Dr. Idris for a pregnancy test. I'm a few minutes late," she said as she looked at her watch.

"Oh, don't worry about it. It's a light day today. We don't have many clients here waiting. I will take you into Room 2. You will find everything you need next to the sink. The restroom is at the end of the hall. Take your sample back into the room with you when you are done. Dr. Idris will be in about ten minutes if not sooner."

"Thanks, Sheila."

Teri quickly collected the specimen cup and walked down the hall to the restroom. She hadn't given a lot of thought to what was going on with her body, but now being there in the doctor's office really brought out the reality of the possibilities, and they all seemed too real. *This may really be happening*, she thought.

After Teri returned to Room 2 with her urine sample, she waited for Dr. Idris to arrive to administer the test. When Dr. Idris entered the room, she was happy to see her friend and colleague.

"Hey, Teri!"

"Hey, Sharon." The two doctors hugged briefly.

"So, you need a pregnancy test I hear," Dr. Idris said with a smile. She rejoiced about motherhood. It was one of the most awesome gifts the human race could experience, in her opinion.

"Yes, I do. How long will it take?"

"I will do the early pregnancy test with a portion of your sample, which will only take a few minutes. Then, I will also run a more thorough test. Are you ready?"

"Sure. I guess so."

"Well, how do you feel about the possibility?"

"Anxious and nervous."

After administering the early pregnancy test, Dr. Idris asked, "Have you mentioned the possibility to Reggie?"

"Not yet."

"Why not?"

"If I'm not, he will be disappointed. He has been waiting for this for quite some time. I want to be 100% sure when I tell him," Teri explained.

"Well," Dr. Idris began, "let's see what the result is," she said as she allowed time for the test stick to change from white to either blue or pink. Teri sat waiting on the table with her hands clasped together. As she sat there, she thought about Reggie and how he had been requesting for the last couple of years for them to add a baby to their family. At the time the requests began, Teri wasn't ready; she had only been on her job for four years. She had wanted to be on her job for at least five years before she took extended time off. She did not want her job status to be jeopardized by not being there. She wanted to establish a firm foundation and have Carte Blanche when and if she needed time off. Now, four years later, she couldn't use the same excuse.

"Well, my friend. It looks like you're going to be a mommy. So, get prepared to tell Mr. Langston he's going to be a daddy."

"Oh, wow," Teri said obviously speechless. "Thanks, Sharon."

"No problem. I will call you tomorrow after I get the other test results."

"Sounds great. I'll check in after my shift or on my break."

Teri left the OB/GYN clinic with butterflies in her stomach. She wanted to plan an evening with her husband to share the news with him, but she wasn't sure if he would be in late or if by chance he would be coming home early for a change. While she understood the demands of his job, it didn't stop her from feeling lonely in their huge home. At the same time, there were nights when she worked late at the hospital, and Reggie was home before she was. So, it all actually balanced out well. She couldn't help to wonder how they would balance their schedules to accommodate the baby. Someone would need to be home with the baby.

When Teri arrived home, she began to look in the refrigerator and the cabinets to see what she could prepare for dinner. As she stood there, she began to feel ill. *Let me lie down for a minute*, she thought. Not really wanting to walk upstairs to the bedroom, she opted to lie on the couch in the family room.

An hour later, Reggie walked in to find Teri asleep. He thought about letting her continue to sleep, but he really wanted to share with her the breakthrough he and the team had made with the shuttle design. So, he went into the kitchen and took from the fridge the remaining salad they had from the night before and served it with the freshly baked pizza he had picked up on the way home.

He placed the meal on serving trays and took it into the family room. Teri, getting a whiff of the pizza, was awakened.

"Hey there, sleeping beauty," Reggie greeted his wife.

"Oh, hey honey. You're home," Teri said half awake. Suddenly, Teri jumped up and raced to the bathroom and emptied the contents of her stomach.

"Baby, are you okay?" Reggie questioned.

"Uh yeah. I'm just pregnant is all," Teri said as she cleaned her mouth.

"Pregnant?"

"Yes, pregnant." When she realized how she just blurted out her special news, she felt silly. That is not at all how she had planned to tell him that he was going to be a father. As Reggie just stood there in near disbelief, Teri tried to clean up her blunder. "Sorry, this is not how I planned to tell you, but it's out now."

"It's okay. Don't worry about that," he said still trying to come to grips with his longtime dream coming to pass. "Well, come have a seat. Are you feeling okay?" Reggie asked immediately going into protective husband, expectant father mode.

"Yes, just experiencing some queasiness. But, I'm fine."

"Okay," Reggie said grinning from ear to ear as he hugged his wife. He had noticed her bouts of nausea, but he figured it would work itself out in time. With him working late hours on the shuttle, he wasn't always around to really notice what was going on. Right now, he just knew he was happy. "Have you told your mom yet?"

"No, I was waiting to tell you first."

"Okay, well I'm going to call Mom and Dad and tell them the good news."

"Okay, I guess I'll call my mom too."

After the phone calls were made, the rest of the evening was spent with the loving couple discussing their future with the new addition to their family. They were both overwhelmed with joy and the anticipation of the months that lie ahead of them. Neither of them had experienced this before, so it would be a journey they could experience together, from beginning to end.

As they sat on the couch half watching television, Reggie broke the quiet and said, "I want the baby to be named after me."

"You mean if it's a boy, right?" Teri asked.

"Boy or girl," he answered.

"I don't know how that's going to work out, but we'll see," Teri said, leaving it at that.

At the end of the week, on Saturday morning, Reggie and Teri decided to begin their day with a walk in the neighborhood park. Because the weather was quite crisp, even though it was technically springtime, they both bundled up with sweatshirts, gloves and scarves. As they walked through the park, Reggie remembered he never shared the news from work with Teri. They were so consumed with the news of the baby that it slipped his mind.

"I have some good news," Reggie announced excitedly.

"Oh, yeah? Okay, share," Teri said with equal excitement. Reggie and Teri always celebrated with one another when they had good news to share. God had blessed them both with lucrative careers, a beautiful home, good health, and a loving marriage. There was no room for jealousy or competition.

"We are done constructing the prototype. It will be tested next week. We will find out what components need to be de-bugged or replaced, if any."

"That's great, honey. And you guys are on schedule?"

"Yes, we are on schedule, but that is not the extent of the good news," Reggie said smiling.

"Okay, well don't hold back. Tell me," Teri said swinging around Reggie like a little girl who had too much sugar.

"I will be on the team of engineers who gets to test the shuttle," Reggie said softly, looking intently at Teri.

"What do you mean 'test' the shuttle? Do you mean you're going into space?" she asked with great concern. Suddenly, she stopped moving about him. Her feet were squarely planted in front of him, and she was looking intently into his eyes. Throughout all the time they dated and during their nearly nine years of marriage, Teri had never been concerned about Reggie being an engineer for *NASA*. This, however, concerned her. The only things that ran through her mind at the moment were the deaths that had occurred in connection with space travel. Both astronauts and even a civilian had died due to attempted space travel in shuttles. She wasn't so sure about this.

"Well, we won't actually travel to the moon, but we will take the shuttle up to test the atmospheric pressure in the cabin."

"So, exactly how far *up* must you go to do that?"

"A little higher than airplanes travel."

"Is there anything I really need to be concerned about? Is this more dangerous than travelling by airplane?"

"Anytime an aircraft has never been tested, there is always inherent danger. BUT, there is no need for alarm. We did not create an entirely new shuttle. What I mean by that is many of the mechanisms are the same, while other parts are new to the space shuttle but have been used on other types of vehicles."

Teri just looked at Reggie. She didn't really know what to say, but she believed what he told her. Yet and still, she had another concern, "The more I think about this, the more I remember about the past. Wasn't there one space shuttle that never made it into space? As a matter of fact, they never made it off the launch pad."

Not wanting to delude his wife, Reggie answered, "Yes, baby, you are correct. That was the Apollo I Rocket."

"And then there was the one that the school teacher was on with the six astronauts. They weren't even off the ground for two minutes, and there was a massive explosion that killed all of them. Reggie, I don't think I like this at all."

"Baby, I truly understand your concern. But it is our job at *NASA* to create and test what we have created before the astronauts can safely use the shuttles."

"And it's no guarantee that the engineers or the astronauts will actually be safe," Teri said interrupting him.

"You're right. We are similar to police officers who get wounded in the line of duty. They risk their lives to protect the lives of others. But, I'm not trying to alarm you, and obviously I can't promise you all will be absolutely fine, but it is our prayer that it will be. I'm just asking you to stand by me as I complete my assignment."

Teri hesitated for a moment. She really didn't know what to say, but she felt deep down she did not want to be selfish. She knew this was every *NASA* engineer's dream. She didn't want to get in the way of her husband's desires. But, she couldn't help but to feel selfish for herself and their unborn child. She wanted her husband with them every step of the journey. And, she wanted him to be whole, not wounded or maimed.

As she was thinking everything through, she walked away from Reggie. He allowed her to move slightly down the path and clear her mind. He wanted her to have a chance to think. He wanted her to come to terms with his assignment, but at the same time, he knew he couldn't force her to accept it. He just hoped she would.

Slowly, Teri turned back around and walked back to her husband. She looked up into his eyes and said, "Okay, honey. I know this means a lot to you. I wish you the best." Reggie breathed a sigh of relief as his wife placed one arm around his waist and they continued on with their walk. "Just don't leave me husbandless and our baby fatherless," she added.

"I will do my very best," he said. And, she knew he meant it.

7

On Monday morning, just as Teri opened the door to the garage to go to her car to head over to the hospital, the doorbell rang. Hurriedly, she answered the door without even looking through the peephole. Standing in front of her was a well-dressed middle-aged man.

"Yes, can I help you?" Teri asked.

"Teri Langston?"

"Yes?"

"You've been served," the man said and handed Teri an envelope.

"Served?" Teri said half to the man and half to herself as she looked down at the envelope she held loosely in her hand. When she lifted her head again, half expecting an answer to her question from the process server, she saw the back of his head as he disappeared down the driveway.

Having only ten minutes to spare, Teri quickly opened the envelope and saw she was listed as the defendant in a lawsuit. The plaintiffs were listed as Jose Chavez and Maria Chavez.

"Oh, my God!" Teri exclaimed. As she read further, she learned she was being sued for medical malpractice and was being labeled as the cause for Jessica's inability to walk. Tears immediately fell from Teri's eyes, and she fell down on the couch with the wind totally gone from her lungs. She couldn't think straight. She didn't know what to do first. *Should I call the hospital? Should I call Reggie? Should I call my mother?*

Trying to compose herself to deal with the devastating change of events. Teri grabbed a Kleenex from the coffee table. When she reached for the phone, trying to decide whom to call first, her phone began to ring. The hospital's main number showed up on the caller ID.

"Dr. Teri Langston," Teri said as she attempted to keep her voice from shaking.

"Dr. Langston, this is Melanie. I am the executive assistant for the chief of staff Dr. Melvin Brown, here at Kaiser Permanente. He would like to speak with you in person immediately. How soon can you come in?"

"May I ask what this is regarding?" Teri asked.

"Dr. Langston, Dr. Brown did not give me the specifics. He just asked me to kindly give you a call. Can I tell him what time you are available, please?" Melanie asked, remaining strictly professional.

"I'm actually headed to the hospital now for my shift."

"Dr. Brown is requesting you come directly to his office upon your arrival, prior to starting your shift. Will you be able to do that, or do you having any pressing appointments with clients that will prevent you from doing so?"

"No, I don't have any pressing appointments," Teri said dryly. She didn't like the feel of being interrogated.

"So, we will see you in about an hour, Dr. Langston?" Melanie continued to press.

"I'll be there within the hour," Teri confirmed.

"Thank you, Dr. Langston. I will apprise Dr. Brown of your arrival time."

"Very well."

Teri's hand was shaking so badly, she could hardly disconnect from the call. She began to replay the surgery in her mind over and over again. She couldn't imagine anything that she could have possibly done to impair Jessica's ability to walk. The bullet entered the skull at the base of Jessica's head, just above the neck, and damaged the cerebellum. What Teri had done in the surgery had saved Jessica's life. *It was the fault of the shooter that Jessica needed surgery in the first place,* Teri thought. *Why am I being sued? I'm not the one who shot her.* Thoughts continued to run rapidly through Teri's mind. And the more she thought, the more infuriated she became. *If they want a fight, I will give them a fight,* she thought.

Teri walked into the kitchen and took out a bottle of cold water. She drank half of it in one gulp and was tempted to splash the other half of it onto her face to see if she was really awake and not having a bad dream. But, she thought better of that idea because she did not want her makeup to run down the front of her Marc Jacobs suit. She had opted to dress in full business attire today because she was not scheduled in surgery. She only had consultations with patients whom she wanted to consider surgery to cure their current ailments. Having cleared her mind, she downed the other half of the water and placed the bottle in the recycling bin.

Making her way to the garage once again, Teri started her car, placed the phone in its holder, and dialed her husband's telephone number. Her call went directly to voicemail. Disappointed, she disconnected from the call without leaving a message and immediately dialed her mother's number.

"Hi, sweetheart," her mother answered.

"Hi, Mom," Teri said crying again.

"Teri, what's wrong?" her mother asked, hearing the distress in her daughter's voice.

"Mom, I'm being sued for medical malpractice."

"Medical malpractice? For what, Teri?"

Teri filled her mother in on the details of Jessica's surgery, the physical therapy, and her inability to walk. Things just didn't add up for Priscilla, Teri's mother.

"Darling, let me call your cousin William to have him look into this case. I'm sure the shooter is probably in custody if he was caught. I will call you back in a bit, or I'll have Will call you."

"Okay, Mom."

"Don't worry, honey. Everything will work out."

"Thanks, Mom."

Teri continued her drive to the hospital. Upon her arrival, she went directly to the chief of staff's office and introduced herself to Melanie.

"Good morning, I'm Dr. Teri Langston. I believe we spoke on the phone this morning," she said to the woman sitting behind the large walnut executive desk.

"Yes, Dr. Langston. I'm Melanie. We did speak this morning. It is nice to meet you in person."

"Thank you. Is Dr. Brown available?"

Melanie lifted the phone receiver and paged Dr. Brown to alert him of Dr. Langston's arrival. He cleared her entrance.

"Yes. Go on in, Dr. Langston. He is expecting you."

It was very difficult for Teri to keep herself composed, but with every ounce of strength she had, she managed to keep her composure in front of strangers, patients, and colleagues. The last thing she wanted to do was to be in the presence of others. She just wanted to be alone, at home, in her bed, under the covers.

As Teri entered Dr. Brown's office, he removed his glasses and rose from his seat. As Teri approached his desk, attempting to make her way to one of the chairs in front of his desk, the tears once again fell from her eyes. Dr. Brown walked over to meet Teri. He embraced her, as he kissed her on the cheek. He held onto her for several moments without saying a word. As she felt the security of his strong arms, Teri allowed herself to be enveloped in his strength. She allowed the tears to flow freely as she sobbed softly against his chest.

"I know, Teri. I know," he said softly in her ear. Teri held onto him as she continued to weep. "Come over here and sit down. Before we discuss the details, let me say this- you know I'm not going to let anything happen to you, don't you?"

Teri nodded. Melvin is Reggie's best friend. He and his wife Trina are family to Reggie and Teri. Over the years, after Melvin and Trina were married, Trina and Teri really hit it off. Trina is the sister Teri never had.

"Have you spoken to Reg about this?" Melvin asked.

"No, I think he's testing the shuttle right now. He didn't answer his phone. I'll talk to him about it later. So, Mel, tell me. What happens now?"

"Well, as you know, it is hospital policy to place you on administrative leave until this issue is resolved. You will continue to receive your pay through your malpractice insurance, but you will not be able to see, treat or have any discussions with any of your patients. I will assign another doctor to see to their well being."

"Understood. Will I at least have an opportunity to introduce the replacement doctor to my patients?

"Unfortunately, you can't have any further contact with your patients *once* I read the subpoena."

Teri's eyes opened wide with Mel's last statement and his emphasis on the word 'once.' "Have you read the subpoena yet?" she asked, to make sure she clearly understood his gesture.

"What subpoena?" Mel answered.

"Thanks, Mel," Teri said. "I'll make my rounds quickly, then I will leave. Tell Trina I'll call her later or tomorrow."

"Will do."

"Oh, Mel. Does Melanie know anything about this?"

"I haven't said anything to her. I haven't said anything to anyone yet."

"Okay, thanks again."

"We will talk later."

Teri quickly made her rounds to her patients and let them know she would be taking a short vacation. Afterward, she got back into her car and drove back home, in tears and disbelief that she was experiencing accusations from the Chavez family.

When she arrived home, she pulled into the garage and saw Reggie's car. *What is he doing home in the afternoon*, Teri wondered. When she walked through the door, Reggie was standing there. He must have heard the garage door open.

"Honey, what are you doing home?" Teri asked.

"Mel called and your mom called. I'm here for you, babe. Where did you think I would be at a time like this?" Teri didn't answer. She let her purse fall to the floor, and she fell into her husband's arms. Reggie slowly walked his wife into the kitchen. Once she was seated, he poured her a glass of cold water. She drank all of it without stopping for a breath of air.

"Honey, I spoke to your cousin Will. He said the shooter is not in custody..."

"Why not?" Teri interrupted.

"Baby, stay calm. Let me finish," Reggie said as he caressed Teri's arm. "He was killed by the police. After he fired the shot that hit the little girl, the police were given a description of the vehicle. There were police units in the vicinity. They caught up with the guy right away and fired shots when the shooter exited his vehicle with his gun drawn. It was basically ruled 'suicide by cop.'"

"So, the Chavez family is coming after me because they can't sue the dead shooter."

"Yes, that's what it sounds like."

"I need to call a lawyer."

"Mel said the hospital will take care of that. All you have to do is prepare for the court date. The lawyer will call us in a few days after he is fully brought up to speed on the case."

"How do I prepare for the court date when I don't know what I supposedly did wrong?"

"Baby, I don't know, but I'm sure your lawyer will explain everything to you."

"I see," Teri said in a fog.

"Honey, don't worry." Then, trying to change the subject, Reggie asked, "What have you eaten today?"

"Um," Teri said trying to remember. "I don't think I have eaten anything. Um, I think I had a banana and a granola bar this morning before the process server came."

"Try to eat something. I want you to try to stay calm. Don't forget about the baby. You don't need to get yourself upset."

Teri managed to eat a half a sandwich and drink a tall glass of warm milk. The milk soothed her nerves and relaxed her. At her husband's suggestion, she went upstairs to take a nap to take her mind momentarily off the situation at hand. Knowing she had family and friends who truly loved her and cared about her well being made her feel a little better. She knew whatever the outcome she would not have to experience it alone.

8

While Teri slept, Reggie cleaned the kitchen and went to the garage to work on his 'project car.' Working on the '64 Chevy Impala soothed him. As he played around with the radio, trying to tune it to a station that would actually come through in the garage, he thought about Teri. She really loved what she did. She loved people, and she would never want to hurt them. He hoped this situation didn't leave her with a sour taste for medicine in her mouth.

Just as Reggie was getting into the groove of replacing the Chevy's carburetor, the doorbell rang. Making his way from the garage, he grabbed a towel to open the door with. He knew if Teri saw oil on the door, he wouldn't hear the end of it. Thinking of his wife and her persnickety ways, he laughed to himself.

When Reggie opened the front door, he was pleasantly surprised to see his best friend since their college days standing at the door with his wife. Mel and Trina didn't usually come by until the weekend. Obviously, they were there for Teri.

"Hey, you guys. Come on in," Reggie said greeting his friends warmly.

"Hey, Reg," Melvin and Trina said in unison.

"Where's my girl?" Trina asked once she had come in and removed her coat.

"She's taking a nap. Go on upstairs."

"I don't want to disturb her," Trina hesitated.

"Oh, she'll be glad to see you," Reggie encouraged. "Mel, come with me into the garage. I'm working on my car."

"The Chevy?"

"You know it," Reggie laughed.

"How's it coming along?"

"Come see for yourself."

While the guys were outside, Trina went upstairs to see about Teri. Teri was sleeping soundly and emitting a little raspy snore. Trina couldn't help but to laugh at the sound of her friend sleeping. Feeling someone's presence in the room, Teri slowly lifted her head from the pillow.

"Girl, what are you doing here?" Teri asked Trina in a drowsy tone.

"Well, Mel and I came by to see how you are, but at the moment I was listening to you raise the roof," Trina said laughing.

"Oh, girl. I know. Reggie told me I snore when I'm really tired. I have been exhausted lately. I guess it's due to the pregnancy, and the news I received today has me emotionally drained."

"I understand. So, on that note, we are going to focus on something else."

"Like what?" Teri asked sarcastically.

"Well," Trina thought, "how about the Sardowsky twins?" The Sardowsky twins are well known in their community because of their antics and their hair-brained schemes. They are also known as the Barbie twins. They bleach their hair and have had every surgery known to women to look like the infamous Barbie doll. And, no one better not attempt to tell them they don't look like Barbie. And because they were born identical twins, whatever surgery one has, the other has also, so they can continue to be identical. All the women around town get a big laugh from them, but the men act like love sick puppy dogs staring after them when they walk by.

"The Sardowsky twins? What are they up to now?"

"Girl, you are not going to believe this."

"I'm sure I will. Nothing they do surprises me anymore after Bam tricked Kam's husband into sleeping with her by pretending to be her sister," Teri said with a smirk.

"Yeah, that was completely nasty, and I am surprised they have continued to speak to each other after that."

"Yeah, me too."

"But, try this on for size. Bam and Kam pretended Bam's daughter had been kidnapped to make Bam's ex-husband appear to be an unfit father, so Bam could get full custody of their children."

"What?!"

"Yes! Kam's boyfriend was in on it too. He snatched the little girl from her father's house when he was otherwise engaged with his new girlfriend and took her to an abandoned warehouse and kept her there until the ransom drop was made."

"So, they actually got away with it?"

"Actually, they almost did. But, Kam's boyfriend made a stupid mistake."

"Oh, really? What was that?" Teri asked completely involved in the story.

"He went to one of the local burger stands and ordered his specially designed burger, which he took with him to the warehouse."

"Okay, how was that a problem?"

"He left the wrapper there. The police found it, took it to the lab to test the ingredients, and traced the burger right back to him."

"You mean to tell me no one else orders their burgers like him from that place?"

"How many people do you know who order their burgers rare with an over-easy fried egg, relish, avocado, bacon, and ketchup on a whole wheat bun?"

"Hum, I see your point. So, the three of them are facing jail time?"

"I would say so. They will be going to trial soon."

"Maybe I will see them around the courtroom," Teri said sarcastically with sadness in her eyes.

"I'm sorry. I came here to cheer you up and take your mind off of everything."

"It's okay. I enjoyed the laugh."

"So, sis. How far along are you?" Trina asked with another attempt to take Teri's mind off the lawsuit.

"I'm about two months."

"Two months and you are just finding out?"

"Yes, well my cycle has been irregular ever since I can remember. So, if I miss a month here or there, I don't think much of it."

"So, what made you take the pregnancy test?"

"I started being nauseous."

"Oh, yeah. That will do it every time. Ok. So, you are two months. That's good. I have a while before I need to begin planning the baby shower."

"Baby shower? Yeah, we have a while before we need to talk about that. But, what we should talk about is dinner. Are you guys able to stay?"

"Yeah sure. How about we order out for pizza?"

"Oh, no! The last time pizza was brought into this house, I got sick."

"Okay. Pizza is definitely out. What about Mexican?"

"I guess I can handle that. I won't know until it gets here."

"Okay, let me check with the men and see what they want. I'll be right back."

Having agreed on Mexican food, the four friends sat around reminiscing about old times as they ate their dinner. They laughed and momentarily took Teri's mind off the lawsuit.

9

Thirty days later, near the beginning of April, Teri sat before Judge Stottlemeyer at the defendant's table. It is customary that the plaintiff presents its case before the judge, detailing the supposedly convicting evidence before the defendant has an opportunity to refute the supposed evidence. So, Teri had to endure sitting quietly as she listened to the evidence against her. Witness testimony after witness testimony seemed to place more and more nails in her metaphorical coffin. The case against her seemed almost airtight.

Those who were chosen to testify against her were an utter surprise to Teri. She never would have guessed that those who were closest to her in the surgical room would be the ones to take the plaintiffs' side. She wondered if they really believed what they were saying.

First, there was Nurse Martha Peterson. When Martha took the stand, the Chavezes' lawyer Sabrina Sherwood asked her to describe Dr. Langston's composure and countenance on the day of Jessica's surgery. Martha began with this, "I have worked with Dr. Langston in the surgical room on many occasions, but this time was a little different."

"Continue Ms. Peterson. Explain what you mean by a little different," Ms. Sherwood encouraged.

"When she entered the room and stood before the table, a tear fell from her eye. Also, she did not begin right away. She stood there for several minutes just looking at the patient."

"Thank you, Nurse Peterson. No further questions."

"Cross examination?" Judge Stottlemeyer asked.

"Yes, Your Honor. I have a few questions. Nurse Peterson, you are here today because you believe Dr. Langston to have been negligent in the medical care given to Jessica Chavez?" Mr. Stephen Peevey, Teri's lawyer, said as he rose from his seat.

"I didn't say those exact words."

"Well, what is your position? You obviously think something must have gone wrong due to your position as the plaintiffs' witness. You stated Dr. Langston shed a single tear. Did this one tear cause her to be unable to see?"

"No, it did not. One of the attendants wiped it away."

"Did another tear fall?"

"Not to my knowledge."

"Nurse Peterson, how long have you assisted in surgical procedures?"

"For well over thirty years," Martha said proudly with her chest puffed up.

"In your thirty plus years have you ever seen a doctor cry?"

"Oh, yes."

"And were any of the other doctors sued for negligence?"

"Not to my knowledge."

"Do you consider Dr. Langston a good surgeon?"

"Yes, I do."

"What about an excellent surgeon?"

"Yes, I do, but even excellent surgeons can make mistakes," Martha offered.

"What mistake do you purport Dr. Langston made while operating on Jessica Chavez, Nurse Peterson?"

"I don't know. I just know she didn't seem to be herself and anything could have gone wrong."

"But, there is no physical evidence to support what you are saying. Isn't that correct?"

"Well, I can't put my finger on it."

"Also, Nurse Peterson, you stated Dr. Langston did not begin the procedure right away. Is that correct?"

"Yes, as I stated, she just stood there looking at the patient."

"By your statement, am I to assume seeing a two-year-old child with a gunshot wound in the back of her head and blood stuck to her hair is not supposed to affect anyone?" Mr. Peevey questioned.

"No, I'm not saying that. I guess anyone would be affected by that."

"You guess anyone would be affected by that? Okay, how did the other attending personnel react when they saw Jessica?"

"Objection, Your Honor. Relevance," blurted out Ms. Sherwood.

"Where are you going with this line of questioning, Mr. Peevey?" Judge Stottlemeyer asked.

"Nurse Peterson appears to be singling out Dr. Langston's initial response to Jessica and linking it to a possible cause of something going wrong during the surgery. I want to know if there was anyone else who had the same reaction, or if Dr. Langston's response was indeed different," Mr. Peevey answered.

"Objection overruled. The witness may answer the question," Judge Stottlemeyer responded.

"Many of them shed tears and were simply horrified by the tragedies children endure at the hands of criminals."

"So, Nurse Peterson, you openly admit there were others who responded in like kind to Dr. Langston's response, but you are finding fault with her for showing human emotions, but not with the others. So, are you stating it is okay for others to show human emotion, but it is not okay for Dr. Langston who is also human to show human emotions?"

"No, I am not saying that at all," Martha said looking and sounding very frustrated for having gotten herself tangled up into giving the testimony that she gave.

"No further questions, Your Honor."

As Nurse Martha Peterson exited the stand, she walked by the plaintiffs' table and gave Ms. Sherwood an evil glance as if to say, "You didn't do a good job protecting me as your witness!" Ms. Sherwood did not acknowledge Ms. Peterson's look. She just kept looking straight ahead.

The next person to take the stand was an attendant, Robbie Showman. Robbie was the attendant who met Teri upon her arrival to the hospital. He assisted her in the sterilization process by placing the gloves on her hands. When Ms. Sherwood asked Robbie to describe his experience in the sterilization room, he said, "Well, when Dr. Langston arrived, she was visibly shaken, and it was obvious to me she had been crying."

"Objection! Speculation on the part of the witness," Mr. Peevey yelled at that point.

"Sustained," Judge Stottlemeyer responded.

"Did you witness anything else, Mr. Showman?" Ms. Sherwood asked as she continued to prod the witness for more ammunition to use against Teri.

Robbie continued, "Yes, as Dr. Langston was washing her hands, I heard her talking to herself. There were no other doctors or nurses in the room, and I was over by the cabinet retrieving her surgical gloves. When I asked her who she was talking to she didn't respond."

"Thank you, Robbie. No further questions," Ms. Sherwood said.

"Cross examination, Mr. Peevey?" Judge Stottlemeyer offered.

"Yes. Thank you, Your Honor. Mr. Showman, you stated Dr. Langston appeared to have been crying when you saw her?"

"Yes."

"Did she have tears running down her face or was she using a Kleenex to wipe her eyes?"

"Uh no," Robbie said slowly.

"Well, what evidence do you have that makes you think she had been crying when you yourself stated you did not see any tears?"

"Her eyes were red. When people cry, their eyes turn red."

Robbie's statement sounded so ridiculous that people in the audience began to laugh, while the jurors had to choke their laughter back.

"Quiet in the court room," Judge Stottlemeyer responded. "Anyone who cannot keep his or her composure will be asked to leave. Please continue, Mr. Peevey."

"Thank you, Your Honor. Mr. Showman, is it possible, from your experience with life, that her eyes could have been red from being asleep?"

"Yes, I guess so, but..."

Mr. Peevey did not bother to allow Robbie to utter another silly explanation for Teri's red eyes or the fact that he really thought it was due to crying. Once he received the answer he was looking for, he continued on with his next question.

"Mr. Showman, were you aware that Dr. Langston had recently been napping when she was summoned to the hospital for the emergency surgery?"

"Uh no. I didn't know that."

"But, you do agree that a person's eyes could be red from sleeping?"

"Yes, I have known that to happen."

"So, we really have no way of knowing what caused the redness in Dr. Langston's eyes if they were indeed red. Do we?"

"I guess not."

"Also, Mr. Showman, you stated Dr. Langston was visibly nervous. Is that correct?"

"Yes, her hands were trembling slightly. She had problems holding onto the soap. She dropped it several times."

"Is she the only one who has ever dropped the soap in the sterilization room, Mr. Showman?"

"No, but..."

"So, how can you say the soap was dropped due to nervousness if others have dropped the soap? Are they all nervous?"

"No, I wouldn't say that, but I also heard her talking to herself," Robbie retorted.

"Mr. Showman, do you believe in God?"

"Objection! Relevance, Your Honor?" Ms. Sherwood interjected.

"Mr. Peevey, is there a point to your question?" Judge Stottlemeyer asked.

"Yes, Your Honor, and I am getting to the point right now."

"Overruled. Let's move this along."

"Yes, I believe in God," Robbie answered.

"Is it possible Dr. Langston was praying?"

"I guess."

"Have you witnessed others praying as they prepared for surgery before?"

"Yes, several doctors do it."

"So, why would you assume Dr. Langston was talking to herself and not God?"

"I couldn't hear what she was saying."

"So, instead of assuming she was praying, it is easier to say she was talking to herself?" Without waiting for Robbie to respond, Mr. Peevey continued, "No further questions for this witness, Your Honor."

"Thank you, Mr. Peevey. You may step down Mr. Showman. The plaintiff may call its next witness."

A few other witnesses were called to the stand and questioned by both sides. Their testimonies were along the same lines as the testimonies of Nurse Martha Peterson and Robbie Showman. Each witness shared his/her own interpretation of Teri's disposition on the night of the surgery. However, not one of them could present a string of patterns Teri had demonstrated in the past. They all confirmed their opinions of her to be a good surgeon and caring doctor, despite the comments they made on the stand.

Finally, Ms. Sherwood said, "The prosecution rests, Your Honor." Teri let out a sigh of relief. She wasn't sure she could listen anymore or hold her composure. She was utterly surprised at the depth of the case the Chavezes' lawyer had built against her. But what was even more surprising was that the shooter was not even once brought into the equation from Ms. Sherwood.

After the plaintiffs' lawyer rested their case, Judge Stottlemeyer adjourned court for the day. The trial would resume the next morning.

As Teri made her way out of the courtroom, she attempted to make eye contact with Mr. and Mrs. Chavez to get a sense of what they were feeling, to see if they had any remorse for dragging her name through the mud. But, just like the last time she saw them in the hospital, they refused to make eye contact with her or even look in her direction. She couldn't help to wonder if they really believed she was the cause of their daughter's inability to walk. She wondered if it was their idea to sue her or if someone else put them up to it. Maybe she would never know the answer to the questions that plagued her mind.

10

Once Reggie heard the testimonies that had gone forth throughout the day, he was glad he had decided to take some time off work to be able to go to court with his wife. He could only imagine what hearing the testimonies did to Teri's spirit. While he stood by her side, another engineer would replace him on the team that was currently testing various safety features of the space shuttle.

When the judge announced the adjournment after the plaintiff had rested, Reggie and Teri walked to the car, while dodging the press' video cameras. Teri was emotionally drained. All she wanted to do was go home and rest. But, Reggie thought it would be best if she ate first. They had been in court for the greater part of the day. Although they were given an hour break for lunch, neither of them was hungry, so they let the time pass by making idle chitchat.

"Babe, let's pick up something to eat on the way home. What do you have a taste for?"

"I don't know if I can hold anything on my stomach. I've been nauseous all morning."

"Do you think it's the pregnancy or bad nerves from the trial?"

"I don't know. Both maybe."

"Well, how about chicken soup?"

"That sounds good, but where can we get some besides the grocery store, in a can?"

"I think I know just the place," Reggie said as he picked up his phone. He dialed Priscilla's number. When she answered, he said, "Hey, Mom. How are you?"

"I'm fine. Just sitting here watching the grandchildren. How's Teri?"

"A little sick on the stomach. Do you have any of your famous chicken soup in the freezer?"

"Actually, I made a fresh pot last night for the kids. You guys want some?"

"I think it would be good for Teri. Can we come by?"

"Of course. You know you don't need to ask."

"Thanks. We'll be right there."

In less than thirty minutes, Reggie and Teri arrived at Priscilla's home, where Teri was greeted by her niece and two nephews. After hugging all of them and her mother, Teri and Reggie settled in for a bowl of hot, tasty chicken soup as they filled Priscilla in on the trial. As Teri replayed the testimonies in her mind, she began to feel a knot form in her stomach. Minutes later, she found herself in the bathroom, expelling the soup.

"Teri, why don't you lie down for a while? I'll get you a ginger ale to try to settle your stomach," Priscilla suggested.

"Okay, Mom. I'll be in my old room." Teri walked into her childhood bedroom and looked around. She had some fond memories of her room, such as coming home and finding new books on her bed. Her mother knew she loved to read as a child, so she always encouraged Teri's favorite pastime by continuing to keep her supplied with new books. Also, Teri remembered the day she came home and found that her mom had painted her room. It was a bright yellow and on one wall, her mother painted shapes. Each shape was a different color. In each shape, Teri hung a small, framed picture.

The room was much different now. Priscilla had re-decorated it for her grandchildren. The room no longer held twin beds. It now holds two sets of bunk beds. Priscilla's grandchildren spend a lot of time at her home because their parents work full time. Those who are too young to go to school spend the entire day with their grandmother, while the other goes to school and comes over afterward.

When Priscilla walked into the room with the ginger ale, she noticed blood on Teri's pants.

"Teri, you're bleeding!" she nearly screamed.

"What!"

"Reggie, come here!" Priscilla yelled. When Reggie entered the room with the young children following behind him, Priscilla said, "Teri needs to go to the emergency room right away. It looks like she's spotting."

"What's spotting, Granny?" one of the boys asked.

"Oh, don't you concern yourself with that," Priscilla answered as she shooed the children out of the room.

"Well, why does Auntie have to go to the hospital?" the little girl asked trying to squeeze between her uncle and her grandmother.

"I'll explain later," Priscilla said, noticing the concern on the children's faces. "Let's go into the kitchen and get a snack," she said to the children to try and distract them from being concerned about their aunt.

"Okay, Mom," Reggie said in response to Priscilla's instructions, as he helped Teri off the bed. "Teri, call your doctor to see if she is on duty right now." When Reggie and Teri got into the car, Teri immediately called Dr. Idris' office. She was not in, but her assistant stated she would attempt to reach her and have her meet them in the emergency room. As they drove to the hospital, Reggie tried to keep Teri calm. She was crying hysterically. *The trial and now this. This is too much for me*, Teri thought.

When they pulled up to the emergency room doors, Dr. Idris was standing there waiting for her friend with a wheelchair. When some of the nurses got wind of Teri being in the emergency room, the word spread. Various hospital staff members were walking by and taking peeks at Teri. They, of course, had all heard about the lawsuit against her. She even overheard one of them say, "I heard her husband works for *NASA*. Maybe this will bring them down to Earth."

On the other hand, there were other personnel who were genuinely concerned about Teri's well-being. They stopped in to check on her and offer words of care and concern. They let her know they were praying for her success in the trial. They also let her know they miss seeing her around the hospital and they hoped she would be back with them soon.

The positive and negative comments had Teri's head spinning. She really couldn't believe there were actually people who wanted to see her fail. The surprise she felt at that moment was the same she had felt in court earlier that day when she listened to testimony after testimony of how she may have been negligent.

Once the attending doctor in the emergency room determined Teri wasn't bleeding heavily and the fetus was in no immediate danger, he released her to Dr. Idris, who moved her to the maternity ward where she could keep a closer eye on her. When Teri was settled into her room, Dr. Idris pulled Teri's medical chart. "Teri, we need to review your medical history as it pertains to pregnancies. I need to know the overall condition of your uterine walls, so I can get a better understanding of why you are spotting. I need to know if this is stress related or something more serious that may come up again."

"Okay, what do you need to know?"

"Have you had any previous pregnancies?"

"Yes, one."

"And, what was the result of the pregnancy?"

"The pregnancy was terminated," Teri said calmly.

"How long ago was that?"

"About twenty or twenty-one years ago."

Teri's answered caused Dr. Idris to stop writing. With her hand suspended in midair, she looked intently at Teri. "That would have made you about fourteen or fifteen years old?"

"Yes, I was fourteen."

"Was the pregnancy a result of consensual sex or rape?"

"Rape," Teri said, still remaining calm and looking directly at Dr. Idris.

"Do you want to talk about it, Teri?"

"No, not really. I've put it behind me."

"Okay, honey. I'm here if you want to talk."

"Thanks. So, what happens now?" Teri asked, anxious to change the subject.

"I need to run some tests, do a pap smear and check the baby's heart rate. Then, I will know how to proceed. I'll have the nurse come in and hook up the fetal monitor to your belly, so we can check on the baby. You just sit tight."

After all the tests were run, it was determined Teri needed to be placed on bed rest for the next seven to ten days to ensure a stoppage of the bleeding. Reggie called Mr. Peevey to let him know Teri would not be in court in the morning because she was in the hospital and would be on bed rest for the next week or so. Mr. Peevey stated he would talk to the judge and try to get a continuance, but he needed Teri's doctor to fax him a medical excuse to present to the judge. Then, Reggie left to go home and pack Teri an overnight bag, so she would have a change of clothes when she was released from the hospital in the next day or two.

Meanwhile, Dr. Idris administered a mild sedative, one that would not harm the baby, so Teri could rest. As Teri began to drift off, she thought about the questions Dr. Idris had asked her about her past pregnancy. She thought about how she lied when she said she had put it behind her. That was so far from the truth. She thought about her unborn child often and had actually calculated how old her child would be if he/she had not been aborted. She thought about how she had no say in the matter. She thought about how it all came to pass and how her innocence was taken from her when she was only a child.

When Teri was fourteen, she walked around the corner from her home to visit Tracy, one of her female friends. When she arrived at Tracy's grandmother's house, Tracy's grandmother notified Teri that Tracy was across the street at her boyfriend's house. Walking across the street, Teri found Tracy and her boyfriend standing outside his front door in a lively conversation.

After some time of just shooting the breeze, the boyfriend said he wanted to show Teri something inside the house. Although Tracy objected to her boyfriend's suggestion, Teri, being naïve, agreed to go inside to see what he wanted to show her. Once inside, Teri found herself being pushed down on an ottoman and her skirt being lifted. Her friend's boyfriend lay on top of her. She tried to push him off, but she was barely five feet, and he was over six feet and very heavy. He laughed and told her to be quiet or her friend who was ringing the doorbell would hear them. He acted as if though it was their secret. Teri did not have a clue as to what was going on, as she was young and inexperienced, but whatever it was he obviously thought she was okay with it.

Before Teri could figure out what was on his mind, he had unzipped his pants, moved her panties to the side and entered into her. She told him to stop and to get off her. She absolutely was not okay with having sex with him. She didn't know him that well, he was her friend's boyfriend, and she wasn't interested in sex.

Instead of taking her objection seriously, he continued on about his business. He was the kind of guy that thought every girl wanted him, and obviously, he wanted to oblige her. He didn't care who the girl was- whether it was his girlfriend, her friend or any other girl. In his effort to finish what he had started, he said, "Wait a minute," with a tone that insinuated it was both their doing. When he finished, after a couple of minutes, he got up, zipped his pants, and went to unlock the door. He laughed and said, "Don't tell Tracy. She might get mad at you." He was taking no responsibility for what had just happened, and he certainly wasn't going to take any blame for it.

When Teri got to the front door, she saw her friend had left. Teri quickly got out of there and never went back to either of their homes again. She was horrified. Never had she had sex, nor had she contemplated having sex. Luckily for her, the rape wasn't brutal. She had no pain, no bleeding, nothing. However, the boy had entered into her far enough that his premature ejaculation entered her cervix, and he impregnated her. But that was not learned until months later when she began to throw up profusely, and her mother took her to the doctor for tests.

Afterward, Teri learned from the doctor that her mother scheduled an abortion. The doctor asked her if it was okay with her, and Teri complied without question. She figured her mother knew what was best for her.

11

The next morning, Mr. Peevey informed Reggie of Judge Stottlemeyer's decision to grant a continuance due to Teri's medical emergency. The defense would present its case in seven days, once Teri was released from bed rest.

Before Reggie drove to the hospital to check on Teri, he decided to pick up her mother. He knew Priscilla was worried about her only daughter and desperately wanted to check on her personally. When Reggie arrived, Priscilla called Betty, one of her friends, to stay with the children. Betty was happy to fill in. She loved children but never had been able to have any of her own.

"I'll only be gone for a few hours, Betty," Priscilla said to her friend.

"Take your time. I'm sure Teri needs you. I'll make the kids a snack, and we will play a game."

As Reggie and Priscilla drove over to the hospital, Priscilla thought about how blessed her daughter was to have such a loving husband. Reggie had come into Teri's life and had taken great care of her. Priscilla didn't have to worry about Reggie mistreating her daughter.

"Mom, what's on your mind? You are very quiet," Reggie said.

"I was just thinking about you, son."

"Oh, really? What about, Mom?"

"It's been over nine years since you and Teri got married. I am so thankful that you are in her life and in our family. You have been such a blessing to all of us."

"That is so kind of you to say. I have been blessed by all of you as well. Thank you for accepting me and my family into your own family."

Upon their arrival at the hospital, they stopped at the gift shop to buy a beautiful bouquet of flowers. When Priscilla and Reggie arrived to Teri's room, Teri was propped up on a set of pillows and was eating applesauce. As soon as she saw her family, her face beamed with joy. Hugs were given all around, and her husband handed her the flowers. She immediately began to sneeze, and her eyes began to water.

"I'll just place these over there on the sink," Reggie said pointing to the other side of the room. Teri just nodded as she wiped her eyes.

"Girl, you are a real mess," her mother said laughing. Teri and Reggie couldn't help but to laugh as well, as they thought about all the different things Teri had experienced since she had become pregnant. Her sense of smell had become intensified, and her taste buds had turned on her. The foods that she always loved to eat, she couldn't eat at the moment. Milk wouldn't stay down. It actually curdled in her stomach, which made it very painful when she regurgitated it.

"Why don't you guys have a seat?" Teri offered.

"What did your doctor say about the bed rest and did you get the results of the tests yet?" Reggie asked.

"All the tests came out fine, except for the stress test. Of course my stress level is high, but that is to be expected with what

I'm going through. But, I must keep my stress level to a minimum because it can severely affect the baby."

"When will you be released?" her mother asked.

"I'll be going home tomorrow, but I will be on bed rest for the next week or so."

"You just make sure you take it easy, dear," Priscilla instructed. "I don't want anything to happen to you or my grandbaby."

"Mom, I plan on taking it easy. Don't worry."

While Teri and her mother were conversing, Reggie turned the TV on and began surfing the channels. Several news stations were discussing Teri's case and even mentioned her being in the hospital. They didn't disclose why she was being hospitalized, but they did mention she had been rushed to the emergency room sometime after the trial had begun on Monday. When Reggie noticed Teri and Priscilla had stopped talking and had tuned into the news broadcast, he turned the channel. He did not want Teri to get upset.

"No, honey. Please, turn it back. I want to hear what spin is being put on the case." When Reggie turned the channel back to the news, a special report was just coming on.

We interrupt our normal news broadcast for a special news report. We are reporting live from Edwards Air Force base here in Los Angeles County, in the city of Lancaster. We have been here for the last week to witness the testing of the newest space shuttle, Forager. Just behind us, the group of engineers is ready for today's test ride. We understand adjustments were made after the last test ride a few days ago. Okay, everyone. Here they go... They are preparing for take-off.

As the shuttle began to rumble and engineers prepared for lift off, the viewers seemed to be holding their breath. Just as the cameras zoomed in for a closer view, the shuttle lifted up and everyone cheered. Not more than three minutes later, the shuttle returned to the ground. The news reporter began to report again.

This is very strange. The shuttle is returning to its starting position. There must be a problem inside the cockpit. We're trying to get someone to answer the radio, but no one is picking up.

Suddenly, the shuttle's door was flung open, and one of the engineers jumped out. There was fire on the back of his uniform. Another engineer jumped out after him and was desperately trying to beat the fire out but was unsuccessful. Finally, a third engineer pulled the second engineer off the first and pushed the first engineer to the ground as he yelled, "Roll, roll, roll!"

Emergency medical personnel were on the scene and immediately moved in with fire extinguishers. The first engineer suffered third degree burns to his back and neck area. The second engineer suffered second degree burns to his hands and forearms.

Reggie, Teri, and Priscilla gasped with surprise and shock as they watched in horror. The same thoughts ran through all of their minds: *It could have been Reggie!* Without saying a word, they grabbed each other's hands. Then, they prayed for Reggie's team members. Secretly, they all were thanking God for protecting Reggie by not having him there.

After all the depressing information they saw on TV, Priscilla grabbed the remote and turned the television off. Reggie immediately stepped into the hallway to call *NASA* to check on everyone. He wasn't able to get any answers because the broadcast was actually being filmed live and no one at headquarters had any information yet beyond what the emergency personnel had already shared about the burns.

A few minutes later, Reggie stepped back into the room just as Priscilla reached into her purse and pulled out her deck of playing cards, and said, "Anybody up for a game of Bid Whiz?"

"Oh, it's on!" Reggie exclaimed.

"Oh, I have this in the bag," Teri said.

"Yeah, we'll see," Priscilla countered.

"What did *NASA* say?" Teri asked her husband.

"They don't have any news. They found out the same way we found out- by watching the live broadcast. I'll check with them again later to get an update on how the guys are doing."

Reggie cleared off the over-the-bed tray, so they could use it as a card table. He sat on one side of Teri, and her mother sat on the other side. They played until Teri's lunch came. It consisted of some type of steak covered in brown gravy, unseasoned mashed potatoes, corn, and Jell-O for dessert. They all looked at it and then looked at each other.

"Who is this for?" Teri asked sarcastically.

"Well, there is only one patient in this room," her mother answered.

"No, I think they made a mistake. I am not eating this," Teri stated in a matter-of-fact tone. She pressed the button for the nurse and requested a plate of fruit. Once it arrived, she happily devoured the fruit.

After Teri ate, Reggie decided it was time to take Priscilla back home and let his wife rest. Plus, he knew Priscilla was anxious to get home to her little rascals.

"Don't think this is over, you guys. I'll beat you guys a little more next time," Teri said with a smile, as she turned over to take a nap.

"Yeah, yeah. I'm going to take your mother home, go by the house and check on some things, but I will be back later," Reggie said as he kissed his wife lightly on the lips.

"Okay, honey. Thanks for bringing Mom by. See you later, Mom."

"See you later, sweetheart. Get some rest. Refrain from having too much excitement."

"I will try," Teri said as she closed her eyes.

12

The next afternoon, Teri was released from the hospital. She and Reggie spent the rest of the day at home relaxing and discussing the chain of events that had transpired over the last few days. They talked about the start of the trial, her experience with spotting, the hospital visit, the fire on *Forager*, and the burned engineers. Teri didn't know what was going on, but she hoped things took a turn for the better. She didn't know if she could take any more bad news. She had already become a nervous wreck. She knew she needed to take it easy and allow her nerves to relax. She needed it not only for herself, but for her unborn child also.

The next day, Reggie returned to work. He figured he would take the opportunity to visit his teammates on the job and in the hospital while his wife was on bed rest. He wanted them to know they had his full support although he was not there with them daily. His first stop was to visit his colleague Tony in the hospital. While he was there, Reggie thought about Tony's family.

"Hey, Tone. How's the family? Do I need to stop by and take Kathy anything?" Reggie asked remembering Tony and his wife have three young children.

"No, man. But, thanks for asking. Her mother and sister take turns going over there to see about them every day." Tony began to grimace from the severe pain he had in his back. Reggie saw the tears well up in Tony's eyes.

"Do you need me to get the nurse?" Reggie offered. Tony only nodded. The pain was so unbearable, he couldn't speak.

Reggie immediately went to the nurses' desk to summon someone to Tony's room. He waited just outside the door as the nurse administered more pain medication intravenously. Although Reggie was large in stature, standing 6'3" and weighing 220 pounds, he was tenderhearted. He did not like to see people in pain. He knew his wife had a compassionate heart too, but he could never do what she did. He wouldn't be able to see hurting people all day everyday entering and exiting the hospital.

After the nurse left Tony's room, Reggie quickly said goodbye and stopped in to see Isaac, whose room was down the hall. Both of his colleagues had rooms in the burn ward. Isaac, with his hands bandaged, was sitting on the edge of the bed. He was being discharged. He and Reggie exchanged a few words. They are not as close as Tony and Reggie are, but Reggie wanted to show his concern to Isaac as well. Tony and Reggie have worked together for about twelve years, while Isaac has only been at *NASA* for six or seven years. Isaac was a private person and kept to himself. He was pleasant, but he didn't really let anyone into his personal space.

After Reggie's visits, he was off to the office.

Back at the house, Teri was sitting in the family room nursing a cup of tea. She was watching the daytime soap opera *One Life to*

Live. Trina was there keeping her company, on her day off. When the segment on the twins came on, Teri was reminded of the latest gossip Trina had shared with her about Kam and Bam Sardowsky.

"So, what's the update on Kam and Bam? How is their court case going?" Teri asked curiously.

"Well, the last I heard, Kam was convicted of conspiracy *only,* because she did not actually kidnap her niece. Kam's boyfriend was convicted of child endangerment, even though it was supposedly a pretend abduction based on the request of the child's mother. Bam was convicted of conspiracy to defraud authorities. None of them were given jail time, but are all considered felons now. And Bam lost custody of all her children to her ex-husband."

"That's a shame," was all Teri could manage to say. She didn't feel bad for them at all. She figured if people engage in idiotic activities, they deserve whatever punishment they receive. *Usually in cases like this, it is the children who really suffer,* she thought.

"Yeah, maybe this will help the twins to grow up," Trina speculated.

"That will be the day," Teri said sarcastically. "Aren't they in their thirties like us?"

"Yes, they are, but they act like they're in their twenties."

"Oh, you are giving them more credit than they deserve. Truth be told, they act like teenagers."

"I've noticed every time I bring them up, you seem to have a hard core attitude about them. Did you ever have a run in with them?"

"Actually, I did. But, it was some years ago."

"Oh, pray tell," Trina said, making herself more comfortable on the couch.

"Well, it was back in my college days, and the three of us went to the same school," Teri began.

"Wait, the twins actually got into a college?"

"Yes, they did. They really aren't as dumb as they act. So, as I was saying, we were in college, and we were all enrolled in the same political science class. You know, one of the required undergraduate classes. Well, we had a test, and Kam decided she would sit next to me. Normally, I sat in the front, and she sat in the back and goofed off. On that particular day, she sat in the front next to me. During the exam, the instructor called us both up and took our tests, tore them up, and dismissed us for the day. He failed us for cheating."

"Oh, my goodness. What did you do?"

"I went straight to the dean and filed a complaint."

"What happened?"

"My grade was overturned, and I was allowed to retake the test. I aced it, of course."

"And, what happened with Kam?"

"She ended up dropping the class."

"Did she ever apologize for getting you involved with her mischief?"

"Of course not. She acted as though she was an innocent victim too."

"That's a shame!"

"Yeah, I know. But what can you expect from trifling folks," Teri said and continued watching the twins on *One Life to Live*.

A few hours later, just as Trina was pulling out of the driveway, Reggie was pulling up. They waved to each other as Reggie's car disappeared into the garage. He was anxious to see his wife. After having been with her all day for the last several days, he missed being in her company. On the way home, he had tried to think of something he could take to her. He knew flowers were out, so he opted for stopping at the corner store and grabbing a bag of gummi bears. Teri loved those sweet little gooey bears. They were one of the few things she could keep in her stomach.

When Reggie walked in, he found Teri dozing away in her Lazy Boy recliner. "Teri," he whispered softly. When she didn't awaken, Reggie moved closer and called her name again.

"Yes, honey?" she said with her eyes still closed.

"I'm home," he responded.

"Okay. Where's Trina?"

"I just saw her pulling away."

"Oh, I must have fallen asleep on her."

"I'm sure she understands," Reggie said as he rubbed his wife's slightly bulging belly. She was now three months pregnant. Although she was at the end of her first trimester, it was still a very delicate time in her pregnancy. In another week, she would be in her second trimester. At that point, Dr. Idris would feel much more at ease with Teri being on her feet. But for now, Teri was instructed to take it easy and to do as little walking a possible, especially up and down the stairs. Following her doctor's instructions, once Teri went downstairs during the day, she stayed down until she was ready for bed. On some days, she didn't go down at all.

"So, honey. How is everything at *NASA*?"

"There is a hold on the space shuttle reconfiguration. They are trying to see what caused the fire. It appears to be either an electrical shortage or a defective part. They will be checking for manufacture recalls on all components used for the cockpit."

"Oh, that's good. Hopefully, they will quickly locate the problem. Can you imagine what would have happened if the fire occurred when the astronauts took the shuttle into space or if the engineers had been a little higher up and not so close to the ground?"

"Yeah, the thought ran through my mind, but I quickly dismissed it."

"Yeah, I understand. It isn't the most pleasant thought. How did your visits go at the hospital?"

"Oh, they went well. I only stayed for a few minutes. I really couldn't bear to see them in pain."

"I know, honey. You're just a big softie," she said as she rubbed her husband's arm.

"Yeah, yeah. You're funny. But, hey, on another note, there was a little tension in the office." Teri's ears perked up. She was always interested in hearing a juicy tidbit here and there.

"Oh, yeah," she said. "What's going on?"

"Well, it appears the drama between Russell and Frank has not been resolved. Russell and Stephanie have still been in contact with one another, and Russell has moved out of his home."

"Oh, really?"

"Yes, and Frank continues to threaten Russell at work about talking to his wife, and Russell doesn't help matters by saying things like 'Well, if you took care of your wife, she wouldn't need to call me.'"

"Oh, those are fighting words."

"Yeah, tell me about it. I just hope they get their acts together before one or both of them ends up without a job. They need to leave personal business out of the office."

With Reggie's last statement, Teri grew quiet. Her mind automatically thought back to a time when she had overheard a voice message from one of Reggie's female coworkers. She was telling him how she was looking forward to seeing him at work the next day. When Teri questioned Reggie about the message and the woman, he admitted the woman had been bringing him lunch and had even offered to cook him dinner at her place. She was a single attractive woman who did not mind one bit if Reggie was married. Teri was disappointed that Reggie had been accepting lunch from her, but at the same time she was happy he had not gone to dinner- to her knowledge. She wondered from time to time what would have happened if she had not overheard the voicemail, and she wondered why Reggie had not mentioned the woman before then.

She was acutely aware that her husband was a good-looking man, but she trusted him unconditionally. He had never given her a reason to doubt his fidelity before that incident, and he tried doubly hard to ensure she didn't doubt him from that point forward. But this drama in the workplace now brought the past back to her remembrance. Getting a sense of where Teri's mind was, Reggie changed the topic.

"So, how are my babies?" Reggie asked referring to his wife and their unborn child.

"We are doing great," Teri said with a genuine smile.

"What game shall we play tonight?" Reggie asked eyeing the stack of games on the card table.

"How about Scrabble or Up-Words?" Teri suggested.

"Sure, as long as you don't use any of those medical terms."

Teri laughed, "All's fair in love and word games."

Playing cards and board games was how Reggie and Teri spent each night while she was on bed rest. After Reggie made it in from work each night, he would prepare dinner quickly if he had not stopped somewhere to pick something up. Teri's stomach was gradually getting stronger. She didn't experience nausea nearly as much. Overtime, she would enjoy her favorite foods again, in addition to the items she craved, such as tuna salad and pastrami.

She had always loved pastrami, but now she actually craved it- almost every other day.

During her time at home, Teri was obedient to her doctor's orders. She did not set foot out the door and did not do too much walking around the house. She really didn't need to because her husband, her friends, and her family were at her beck and call. They were all concerned about her well-being. Some of her coworkers even stopped by to check on her. She was grateful to be well taken care of.

13

Bright and early on the next Monday morning, Reggie rolled Teri in a wheelchair up to the defendant's table. Then, he kissed her on top of her head and took his seat behind her, in the audience. Teri had been released from bed rest, but because it was her first day out of the house and it would be a long day in court, Reggie thought it would be best if Teri did not over exert herself with too much walking or standing.

On the Saturday before, Reggie had placed a call to Melvin to request the special favor of the wheelchair. Melvin readily consented and offered to bring the wheelchair over to their home himself. Melvin's generosity and thoughtfulness saved Reggie a trip to the hospital and spared Teri from once again being gossiped about by the hospital personnel- at least for the time being. People always loved to have something to talk about, even if it was at someone else's expense.

Reggie's plan to diffuse the gossip may have worked at the hospital, but it did not work at the courthouse. The media was well aware that the Langston trial was continuing that morning, and the newscasters were lining the courthouse steps with their cameras when Teri arrived. Mr. Peevey, concerned for his client's safety and health, did his best to shield Teri from the overzealous reporters, as Reggie pushed her up the ramp. The news crews shouted questions, such as, "How does it feel to be unable to walk like Jessica?" "Are you trying to get sympathy from the jury?" "Why were you in the emergency room?"

Teri tried hard to keep her composure, even while listening to them hurl accusations in the form of questions. When she had finally made it into the courtroom, she realized she had been successful, for she had not shed one tear although their negative speculations hurt her to the core. She had allowed her work to speak for itself all these years, and she really didn't appreciate her name and reputation being marred as a result of unworthy newscasters who were making unfounded speculations and unproven accusations.

As everyone waited for Judge Stottlemeyer to take the bench, Mr. Peevey reminded Teri it was okay to show emotion when and if she took the stand. Teri simply nodded, showing she understood. She thought, *How can I not? I am a ball of emotions. I just pray I don't come unraveled.*

A few minutes later, Judge Stottlemeyer entered the courtroom and began to approach the bench. The bailiff asked everyone to stand. Before the judge made his opening remarks, he asked everyone to be reseated. Judge Stottlemeyer quickly reviewed what had transpired in the case thus far; then, he asked the defense to proceed with its first witness.

Mr. Peevey called Officer Steward, one of the officers who was called to the scene of the incident. "Officer Steward, can you describe the incident that occurred on July 18 that involved the shooting of two-year-old Jessica Chavez?"

"Yes, on July 18 in the afternoon, my partner Officer Shawn Brown and I were driving through South Central doing our regular neighborhood patrol when we received a call over the radio regarding a drive-by shooting."

"Did you and Officer Brown respond to the call?"

"Yes, we did."

"What did you find when you arrived to the location?"

"We never made it to the actual location."

"Please explain, Officer Steward."

"When we were in route, another squad car made it prior to our arrival and called for medical attention for Jessica Chavez and the other victim. When the other officers arrived, the suspect was fleeing the scene. They radioed in a description of the car."

Jose and Maria Chavez sat listening to the officer's testimony and suddenly in the midst of the quiet atmosphere, Maria let out a scream. Everyone turned in her direction. Teri looked at the jury members. They all looked sympathetic.

"Ms. Sherwood, is your client going to be okay to remain in the courtroom?"

After quickly conferring with Maria, Ms. Sherwood answered, "Yes, Your Honor, she'll be fine. Thanks for asking."

"Very well," Judge Stottlemeyer responded. "Mr. Peevey, you may continue your line of questioning."

"Officer Steward, what happened when you and your partner received notification of the description?" Mr. Peevey inquired.

"We just happened to be passing through a signal light at the same time as the suspect who was speeding past us going the opposite direction. We immediately made a U-turn and gave chase. Eventually, we caught up with him. When he pulled over, we told the suspect to exit the vehicle."

"What happened then?"

"The suspect exited the vehicle with his weapon drawn. He was warned to put his weapon down."

"Did he comply?"

"He did not. Instead, he lifted his weapon, and he was then fired upon by both my partner and me."

"Were the fired shots fatal?"

"Yes, they were."

"Officer Steward, in your experience as a police officer, have you known the family of a shooting victim to sue the doctor that performed the surgery to remove the bullet?"

"No, usually the suspect is sued."

"So, in this case because the suspect is dead and unable to be sued, the doctor is being used as a scapegoat?"

Ms. Sherwood rose from her chair and said, "Objection. The defense is asking the witness to speculate about the intentions of the plaintiffs."

"Sustained," Judge Stottlemeyer agreed.

"Thank you, Officer Steward. No further questions, Your Honor."

"Ms. Sherwood, cross examination?"

"Not at this time, Your Honor. But the plaintiff reserves the right to call this witness back to the stand at a later time."

"So noted," Judge Stottlemeyer remarked. "Please call your next witness, Mr. Peevey."

Mr. Peevey called Dr. Sharon Idris to the stand. After having her state her full name for the court's record, Mr. Peevey asked Sharon to explain her relationship with Teri.

"I am Dr. Langston's OB/GYN as well as her friend and colleague."

"So you know her in a professional capacity as well as in the capacity of a patient."

"Yes, and I am also a friend of Dr. Langston's," Sharon reiterated.

"Would you say your friendship grew from being colleagues or from Dr. Langston being your patient?"

"Actually, Mr. Peevey, my relationship with Dr. Langston grew as a result of her constantly coming to comfort me after each of my husband's surgeries."

"What type of surgeries did your husband have, Dr. Idris?"

"Objection, Your Honor. What does Dr. Idris' husband's surgeries have to do with Dr. Idris' relationship with Dr. Langston?" Ms. Sherwood interjected.

"I am attempting to show relevance with my current line of questioning," Mr. Peevey responded without giving Judge Stottlemeyer an opportunity to respond to the objection.

"Overruled," Judge Stottlemeyer said looking apparently disturbed by the exchange between the two lawyers. "Continue, Mr. Peevey," he instructed as he leaned back in his chair with his hand on his chin. Judge Stottlemeyer was nearly eighty years old, had graced the bench for over thirty years, and did not like shenanigans. He ran a tight but smooth-sailing courtroom. There was no room for theatrics, and the lawyers were well aware of this.

"Please continue, Dr. Idris. What types of surgeries did your husband have?"

"He had two brain surgeries. He had to have a blood clot removed and a tumor."

"And who was the attending surgeon?"

"Dr. Langston performed both surgeries."

"And were the surgeries successful?"

"Yes, they were. My husband had experienced extreme headaches and had begun to forget a lot. But after the surgeries, he returned to his normal self. Instead of wearing a daily frown, he is happy and smiling again. See for yourself. Stand up, honey." Mr. Steve Idris stood up quickly and waved.

"Uh, Dr. Idris, just answer the questions that are asked of you," Judge Stottlemeyer interjected.

"Sorry, Your Honor," Sharon said with a smile. She and her husband had planned to do exactly as they had just done in an effort to assist Teri in her defense.

"How long ago were your husband's surgeries, Dr. Idris?"

"The first one was about four years ago, and the second one was six months after that."

"Do you recall if there were any complications at all or if there was anything that made you uncomfortable?

"There weren't any complications, but there was one thing that did concern me at the time." Hearing Sharon's response, Teri's back stiffened. Although Teri trusted Sharon explicitly and she appreciated all she had heard thus far, she didn't know if Sharon's testimony was taking a turn for the worse. As she held her breath, she listened intently to what would be said next.

"And what was that, Dr. Idris?"

"Directly after the surgery, the doctors and nurses left the surgical room, but none of them came to inform me of the result of the surgery. I felt neglected."

"Are you stating after your husband's surgery, Dr. Langston did not come out to discuss the results with you?"

"Well, she didn't come out right away."

"Okay, did she eventually come and speak to you?"

"Yes, she did."

"And, at that time did you learn the reason for the initial delay?"

"Yes, I did, and after hearing her train of thought, I have even more respect for her and the work she does for the community."

"Please tell us, Dr. Idris, what caused Dr. Langston's delay?"

"She simply wanted to change her clothing as to not cause alarm to the family members by the amount of blood she had on her clothing. It was simply out of respect, care and concern for us: me and my children."

Dr. Idris' testimony, and the several others that were along the same lines, made Teri's heart warm.

During the afternoon lunch recess, Reggie and Teri had to once again fight through the crowd of spectators, news reporters, and cameramen to get to their car. The judge allowed a two-hour break; this would give everyone an opportunity to refresh him/herself and be ready to continue the case.

Taking advantage of the two-hour break, Reggie drove his wife to the *Soup Plantation*, so she could have her favorite soup: cream of broccoli. That placed a smile on Teri's face. She sat quietly at the table sipping an Arnold Palmer as her husband carried a tray of hot soup and fresh breads to their table. The hot soup warmed Teri's stomach and helped relax her nerves. Reggie was pleased to see his wife eating and not being a ball of nerves.

Back in the courtroom, Mr. Peevey resumed calling his witnesses. His next witness was Dr. Teri Langston, the defendant. Once Teri took her place on the witness stand and stated her name, her lawyer Mr. Peevey began his line of questioning.

"Dr. Langston, how long have you been performing brain surgeries?"

"Nine and a half years."

"Dr. Langston, in the nine and a half years that you have been performing brain surgeries, how many surgeries have you performed?"

"I do not know the exact number, but I venture to say there have been approximately seventy-five."

"In those nine and a half years, have you ever committed an error while operating that caused irreparable damage to someone?"

"No, not to my knowledge. But, I'm sure if I had, I would have known about it."

"Have any of the seventy-five patients complained or sued you for any reason?"

"Only one- the Chavez family, the reason we are in court today."

"Dr. Langston, assessing yourself honestly was there any impediment that would have caused you to be off your mark, to throw your concentration off?"

"Only the fact that the patient was two and a half years old and very small."

"Was this your first time operating on a child?"

"No, but it was my first time operating on a two and a half year old gunshot victim and honestly, it was disturbing."

"So, can we assume the testimonies of Robbie Showman and Nurse Peterson gave about you shedding tears were accurate?

"I did not cry while I was in the sterilization room, but I did shed a single tear when I first stood over Jessica at the operating table." Remembering Jessica's bloody head and the damage the bullet caused to the back of Jessica's skull, a single tear ran down Teri's cheek.

"Dr. Langston, I don't want to upset you. Are you okay to continue?"

"Yes, I'm fine."

"Okay, one final question. To your knowledge, did you make any errors that would have contributed to Jessica's inability to walk?"

"No, I did not. The location the bullet entered Jessica's skull was at the base of the skull called the cerebellum. This is the part of the brain that controls movement. If any damage was caused, the bullet caused it. Also, if there was any damage caused by the surgery, scar tissue would have already begun to form, and it will show on any x-ray."

"No further questions, Your Honor."

"Cross examination, Ms. Sherwood?"

"Yes, Your Honor. Dr. Langston, can you say with medical certainty that the bullet caused the damage and not the surgery you performed?"

"Can you say it wasn't the effect of the shooting?" Teri retorted.

"Dr. Langston, can you please answer the question with a simple yes or no?"

"No." Teri's response caused a hush to fall upon the audience. Everyone waited for the next move.

"No further questions," Ms. Sherwood said and took her seat.

"Your Honor, redirect please."

"Go ahead," Judge Stottlemeyer consented.

"Dr. Langston, why is it that you cannot state with a medical certainty that the surgery did not cause Jessica's inability to walk?"

"I have not seen any x-rays of Jessica's brain. I have only seen CAT Scans, and that was several months ago."

"Thank you, Dr. Langston. Next, I would like to call Dr. Melvin Brown to the stand." After Melvin was sworn in and had stated his name and position at the hospital, Mr. Peevey immediately got to the heart of his testimony and the reason he was called to the stand. "Dr. Brown, it is my understanding the surgery Dr. Langston performed was videotaped. Is that correct?"

"Yes, that's correct."

"Is that standard operating procedure at Kaiser?"

"Yes, it is."

"And, I also understand the video was reviewed by other brain surgeons. Is that correct?"

"Yes, that's correct."

"What were the findings of the team of surgeons?"

"The team consisted of six renowned brain surgeons from around the world, and upon reviewing the tape of Dr. Langston's surgery, all doctors concur that she was not negligent in any shape or form."

"Thank you, Dr. Brown."

"My pleasure."

"No further questions, Your Honor."

"Cross examination, Ms. Sherwood?"

"Yes, Your Honor. Dr. Brown, just a minute ago you stated it was your pleasure to testify on Dr. Langston's behalf. Why is that?"

"Dr. Langston is a fine surgeon, one of the best in the United States."

"Isn't it true you are testifying on her behalf today because you are more than colleagues?" Once again a hush fell over the audience. Melvin, Trina, Reggie, and Teri could not believe their ears. They knew from Ms. Sherwood's very suggestion where her line of questioning was going.

"Objection!" Mr. Peevey interjected, not knowing if Ms. Sherwood's line of questioning would turn up something he had no knowledge of.

"What is the basis of your objection?" Judge Stottlemeyer asked.

"Relevance, Your Honor."

"Goes to motive for the witness' testimony, Your Honor."

"Overruled. Proceed," Judge Stottlemeyer said.

"Please, answer the question, Dr. Brown."

"I'm not sure what you mean by more than colleagues."

"Isn't it true that you and Dr. Langston have an intimate relationship?"

"No, we do not."

"Isn't it true you checked out a wheelchair for her, Dr. Brown?"

"Yes, I did."

"Is it normal hospital policy for the chief of staff to check out a wheelchair for one of the doctors?"

"I did it at the request of a friend."

"Dr. Langston I'm assuming."

"No, not Dr. Langston."

"Isn't it true you requested to see Dr. Langston in your office and when she arrived you embraced her for a while and then kissed her?"

"Yes, I kissed her on the cheek, and I consoled her. This lawsuit has her very upset."

"Is this how you interact with all your staff members? Is this normal operating procedure, Dr. Brown?"

"Look, you are trying to twist everything out of proportion and trying to make something sordid out of it."

"Well, what is the explanation for your behavior, Dr. Brown? Because it sounds as though your intimate behaviors may have affected your testimony today."

"Dr. Langston is the wife of my best friend, and she..."

"No further questions," Ms. Sherwood said, not allowing Melvin to finish his statement.

"Redirect, Your Honor," Mr. Peevey said.

"I'll allow."

"Dr. Brown, please finish your statement."

"Dr. Langston is an excellent surgeon, and her record speaks for itself."

"Thank you, Dr. Brown. The defense rests, Your Honor."

"Ms. Sherwood, are there any further cross examinations or re-directs needed for the plaintiff?"

"No, the plaintiff rests, Your Honor."

At that point, the judge gave instructions for the jury, as they were about to begin their deliberations on all the evidence presented. Court was to stand in recess until such time that the deliberations were complete.

14

Over the next few days, while Teri waited for the jury's verdict, she tried to relax at home and keep her mind off the trial. Her pregnancy was coming along fine, and she was adjusting well to the changes in her moods, her eating habits, and her body. She was finally beginning to show signs of being pregnant in her stomach area and in her face. She was in her fourth month.

While Teri was having lunch and watching *Property Virgins* on HGTV, the doorbell rang. She wasn't expecting anyone, so she was somewhat surprised. As she made her way to the door, the doorbell rang again.

"I'm coming," Teri shouted, getting irritated.

Whoever was at the door was interrupting her show. She was right at the point where the homebuyers were about to decide which house would be the best for them of the several houses they had been shown. She had made her selection, and she was anxious to see if she was correct.

When she opened the door, she found her mother standing there. "Hey, Mom," she said as Priscilla reached in for a hug.

"What are you doing here? Where are the kids?" she asked referring to her niece and nephews.

"I will answer your questions as soon as I get inside out of the cold," Priscilla said as her bottom lip quivered. To be the middle of spring, it was quite cold outside although the sun was shining brightly.

"Sorry, Mom. Come in," Teri said as she moved back out of the way.

As Priscilla stepped into the foyer, Teri took her coat and gloves and hung them in the hallway closet. Meanwhile, Priscilla made her way into the family room with a large paper bag. She knew more than likely that is where Teri was hanging out. When Teri came into the room, her mother handed her a beautifully wrapped box, which she had concealed in the bag. Teri's eyes became very large with excitement.

"Wow! This is for me?"

"Yes, sweetheart. Go ahead and open it." Teri slowly untied the huge bow and carefully removed the tape that held the paper together. Priscilla smiled as she watched her daughter. Teri had always been meticulous and neat. Everything had to be in pristine order. Priscilla wanted Teri to get to the contents inside, but she knew it would be a waste of time to try to rush Teri along. When Teri finally removed the paper, she began to examine the box that held the gift. But the box held no clues as to what was inside. Next, she proceeded to open the box. Inside was a beautiful hand painted silver and gold elephant. It was very exquisite. Teri began to thank her mother over and over again as she continued to admire the piece of art.

"When I saw it, I thought of you. I thought you would like it to go with your other elephants," Priscilla said as she glanced around her daughter's home. Teri had an affinity for elephants. She thought they made great accent pieces for the furniture, and she was right. They added a certain flair to her décor.

After she found the perfect location for her new treasure, she turned her attention back to her mother. "Would you like some hot tea, Mom, or a bowl of soup?"

"Is the soup homemade?"

"Yes, ma'am."

"You mean you actually made soup, Teri?" Before Teri could respond, Priscilla continued, "Well, I guess you do have a little time on your hands."

"Yeah, just a little," Teri said disappointedly. Priscilla noticed a slight change in Teri's mood, and she knew she had touched a sore spot. It was definitely understandable. If Teri was found guilty, the findings would be sent to the Medical Review Board, and her medical license could be in jeopardy. And if that happened, she would have even more time on her hands.

After preparing her mother a bowl of soup, Teri resumed watching her show. She was able to catch the very end of the show and was able to see the homebuyers choose the same home she had selected for them.

At the courthouse, the jurors had been sequestered for the last few days because they had failed to reach a unanimous verdict at the end of the first day of deliberations, which was the day after the defense had rested its case. It is a common procedure for jurors to be sequestered in a hotel. This prevents them from discussing the case with outside parties, watching the news, and receiving other outside influences. Also, the jury is able to spend longer hours together to reach a consensus.

As the jurors reviewed the information from both the plaintiff and the defendant, they came up with varying opinions. One said,

"Dr. Brown's testimony has me a little confused. Do you guys think he and the doc have something going on? Maybe he is covering up something for her."

Another responded, "To be frank, I thought something was going to be revealed with the way Ms. Sherwood was questioning him. I thought at any moment new information was going to be uncovered."

A third juror said, "Ms. Sherwood probably thought something was going on, but she was proven wrong. She was only able to uncover a long friendship. The friendship was probably kept secret because people would frown upon her husband's best friend being her boss."

"Yeah, you're right," the first juror agreed.

"People are always trying to make something out of nothing."

"Yeah and making people look guilty in the process."

The foreman decided it was time to get the discussion back on track. "So, people. Let's focus. Dr. Langston said she couldn't state with a medical certainty whether she or the bullet caused the damage Jessica is currently facing. What does that tell us?"

"It doesn't tell us anything."

"She said she would need to see an x-ray."

"So, can we request an x-ray along with someone's diagnosis of it?"

"No!"

"Well, why not? It may be the missing link to finding who is at fault."

"It was the plaintiffs' responsibility to request an x-ray to prove their case, if the x-ray indeed shows anything to provide proof for their argument."

"Maybe they did see an x-ray and found out they were wrong."

Again the foreman spoke up, "Look, we can't continue with all the speculations and circular language. We must deal strictly with the evidence."

"I agree," another juror stated.

"If we examine Dr. Brown's testimony closer, we will see he shared information from a group of experts that reviewed the taped surgery. They would have been able to see if Dr. Langston had done something wrong."

"Yes, that's true."

"So, their findings may actually be better than having an x-ray."

"At the same time, Dr. Langston admitted she was a little taken aback by Jessica being so young with a gunshot wound."

"And?"

"And, maybe it affected her more than she thought."

"That could have easily been the case, too."

The jurors' conversations went around and around for four days. On Friday evening, the jurors decided to buckle down, focus, write information on the white board, and place their biases aside. They were determined to form a unanimous decision, but they needed to take a dinner break first. Maybe food and a moment of peace and quiet would allow them to think more clearly and focus a little better. They all agreed to take a short dinner break. So to hurry the time along, they ordered pizza. When it came, they stopped for half an hour to eat.

After they sat and ate quietly, some walked out for a cigarette break, while others took a walk down the hotel corridor. They couldn't go too far. Once they reconvened, they stayed focus on their civil duty and left aside all biases.

By the end of the night, they had fulfilled their obligation as jurors in the Chavez vs. Langston Case. For them, that meant they could go home to their families. And, they would not be stuck in the hotel over the weekend.

15

On Monday morning at 10am, Teri and Reggie walked through the crowd of reporters with their heads held high. They had prayed that morning before leaving their home, and they were prepared to stand together no matter what the outcome of the verdict. Teri was determined to stay focused and not allow the reporters' insidious questions shake her. They yelled out, "Do you think you will be exonerated?" "What do you think the verdict will be?" "What will you do if you can no longer practice medicine?"

Once inside, Teri took her usual seat at the defendant's table, and Reggie sat behind her in the audience. Seated next to Reggie were Priscilla, Melvin, Trina, and Teri's brother, Parker.

As Teri sat next to Mr. Peevey, who was looking over his notes, she turned to view her supporters. She was pleased to have such a crowd of supporters who not once questioned her innocence throughout the entire trial. They believed in her abilities and her reputation. For them, her previous surgeries and recognition throughout the medical community spoke volumes. But despite their support, she couldn't help but to feel very nervous and anxious about the jury's findings. What happened in court today could make or break her career.

As Teri was deep in thought, the jury entered the courtroom and took their seats. *Here we go*, Teri thought.

"All rise. Judge Stottlemeyer is approaching the bench. Court is now in session. The case of Chavez vs. Langston will reconvene," the bailiff belted out.

"Today, we are here for the reading of the verdict in the Chavez vs. Langston case. Mr. Foreman, has the juror reached a unanimous verdict in this case?" Judge Stottlemeyer asked.

The foreman rose from his seat, and said, "Yes, Your Honor."

"Will the defendant please rise?" Teri slowly rose to her feet and looked directly at the foreman.

"What is the jury's finding?" Judge Stottlemeyer asked.

A complete hush fell over the courtroom. It was as though everyone was holding in his/her breath. The only noise that could be heard was the heater whirring softly. No one was moving, no one was whispering, and no one was shuffling papers. Teri's hands were tightly clasped on top of the table. She was doing all she could to stay very composed. Priscilla grabbed Reggie's hand and held it tightly. Trina softly laid her head on Melvin's shoulder and closed her eyes. Parker placed his hand on his mother's leg to keep it from shaking against his. Within seconds, the foreman began to speak.

"We, the jury of the people of California, in the county of Los Angeles, in the case of Jose and Maria Chavez vs. Dr. Teri Langston, for the charge of medical malpractice and negligence, find the defendant Dr. Teri Langston to be 'Not Guilty.'"

At the reading of the verdict, Teri's supporters jumped from their seats and let out shouts of joy. Mr. Peevey reached over and placed his arm around Teri's shoulders to congratulate her. Teri's head dropped and tears of joy sprang from her eyes as her small arms encircled her belly and embraced her unborn child. Her tears purified the anxiety she felt within. She couldn't speak. All she could do was nod her head in affirmation. She was completely overwhelmed and outdone by the accusations and the court proceedings. At the same time, she was overjoyed to move past this chapter in her life.

"Order in the court," Judge Stottlemeyer shouted as he banged his gavel.

Immediately, the court returned to its prior quiet state.

"I certainly understand the excitement and joy Dr. Langston and her family must be experiencing right now. It is the very test of human nature to work diligently in a profession and have one's very work challenged by disgruntled clients, customers or patients. Dr. Langston, the charges that have been filed against you in relation to the surgery you performed on Jessica Chavez are hereby dismissed, and you are free to go, with a clean record. I wish you continued success as you continue to save and restore lives. May the grace of God continue to be with you."

Teri slowly rose from her seat and faced the judge. "Thank you, Your Honor," she said with tears yet streaming down her face. That was all she could muster up to say. Judge Stottlemeyer certainly understood.

"Court is adjourned," Judge Stottlemeyer said as he replaced his gavel and exited the bench.

After thanking Mr. Peevey again for his assistance and excellent strategies to bring out the truth, Teri immediately ran into her husband's arms. They all took turns hugging one another and giving each other high fives. Priscilla joined Teri in shedding tears of joy and relief.

"Shall we go out and celebrate?" Reggie suggested once they made their way into the corridor.

"That sounds like it is definitely in order," Melvin agreed.

"I have a table for six reserved at Benihana," Reggie reported. Teri and the others looked at Reggie with surprise. Without waiting for them to verbalize their surprise, Reggie continued. "I knew we would be celebrating a victory today. Didn't you guys?"

"Of course," Trina said.

"Without a doubt," Melvin said.

"Only God knew, but yes, I was hopeful," Priscilla said.

"Well, let's go eat. My treat," Reggie said, as he took his wife by the hand and led her to the courthouse steps. Waiting for them, as they expected, were the numerous reporters.

"Dr. Langston, were you surprised by the verdict today?" one reporter asked while pushing his microphone into her face.

"No, I'm not," Teri replied showing her annoyance with the rudeness of the reporters.

"So, you knew you would be found innocent?"

"Well, I knew I had not done anything wrong when I performed the surgery. I always take great care with my patients," Teri answered with all humility and concern.

"Are there any hard feelings against the Chavez family?"

"No, of course not. I am disappointed in their actions, but I still wish them and their daughter Jessica the best. That is all I ever want for my patients." With her last response, Teri walked away. She had both a feeling of relief, but also one of sorrow because of Jessica's continued inability to walk.

After caravanning over to Benihana, the six of them walked inside the restaurant full of life. Their chatter immediately caught the attention of the restaurant's host. "Good afternoon. Welcome to Benihana."

"Thank you," they all replied in unison.

"You must be here for a celebration," the host observed.

"As a matter of fact, we are," Reggie affirmed.

"Oh, what's the occasion, if you don't mind me asking?"
No one really wanted to state specifically what was going on, so they all stood quietly. As the host looked at each one of them, he took a second look at Teri. After quickly studying her face, he looked up towards the television monitor that was posted in the lobby. Their eyes followed his eyes. There Teri was live in color on the courtroom steps responding to the reporter. The live broadcast was being replayed on one of the local news channels.

Immediately, the host understood their excitement. Not wanting to interfere in Teri's privacy, the host simply smiled and said, "Congratulations. Let me show you to your table, Dr. Langston."

"That would be nice," Teri said smiling and appreciating his show of respect.

Once the group was seated, they ordered champagne and white grape juice for Teri. They toasted to Teri's victory and getting back on track.

"Teri, putting this all behind you, when will you be returning to work?" Melvin asked in his authoritative chief-of-staff voice.

"Oh, honey, give her a break. Can she have a minute to breathe?" Trina fussed.

"It's okay, Trina. Melvin, I don't know. I understand only one of my patients is still in recovery, but the others have been discharged. I guess I can come back in a day or so. Give me a day to absorb everything."

"Fair enough," Melvin said.

As they ate Hibachi Steak, chicken and shrimp dishes, and even sushi for some of them, they laughed and joked. That was something Teri had not done in quite some time. She had been a ball of nerves for the greater part of two months, since she had received the subpoena. Now she felt free, and it showed in her conversation, her facial expressions, and her movements. Priscilla was glad to see her daughter at ease. She was greatly concerned about the well being of her unborn grandchild.

Turning her attention to her only son, Parker, Priscilla noticed he had grown quiet and seemed to be preoccupied with something else. "What is it, son?" Priscilla queried softly as not to draw attention from the others.

"Noel is thinking about divorce."

"What? Why?"

"She said she isn't getting what she needs from the relationship. She says I don't pay enough attention to her."

"Well, do you?"

"Honestly, I know I have been preoccupied ever since I went back to school. But, this is something I am doing for us and our children. I didn't do it to neglect her or them."

"I thought she supported you 100%."

"She did in the beginning, but things have changed."

"It sounds like something else is going on, son. It sounds like she is using your education as a smokescreen for a deeper issue. You need to find out what is going on with Noel, and you need to do it quickly."

"What do you think it is, Mom?"

"I have a feeling you already know," Priscilla said as she looked away from the hurt she saw in her son's eyes. She didn't want to spoil Teri's celebration, and she didn't want to pry in her son's marriage, but she had already had a fainting suspicion that there was trouble in paradise.

16

Now that the court trial had ended, Reggie felt free to return to *NASA*. When he entered the jobsite on Tuesday morning, he immediately went to the senior supervisor to learn what had taken place with the advancement of the space shuttle. When he approached the office door, he overheard two of the supervisors discussing the cockpit fire and the two injured engineers.

"Tony is not going to be able to return to work for a very long time, if ever. The burns to his back caused irreparable nerve damage."

"I understand that, but what about the lawsuit he filed?"

"Well, there isn't going to be a lawsuit. In the engineer contract, there is a clause that discusses inherent danger that comes with the job assignments here at *NASA*."

"Has Tony been reminded of that clause?"

"He will be. Our lawyers are in the process of responding to the lawsuit now. Our primary concern is his health and the well-being of his family. He is still one of us."

"Yes, he is. But, I am curious. Do you think his decision to file the lawsuit was a result of the exorbitant medical expenses or because he believes *NASA* was negligent in the design of the shuttle or the parts that were used that led to the fire?"

"I'm not sure, but if his reasoning is the latter, he would be included in the negligence because he was part of the design team. So, in essence, he would be suing himself as well as us."

"That's true unless he disputed the use of certain materials."

"The tapes of all planning sessions will be reviewed to make sure that is not the case."

"That's wise. Another question: We are covering all medical expenses aren't we?"

"Yes, of course. The hospital was directed to send all medical bills for Tony and Isaac to our office."

Not wanting to feel like a snoop, Reggie interrupted the conversation by knocking at the door. Immediately, the conversation ceased, and Reggie was welcomed into the office. He was quickly brought up to speed on the improvements that were made within the shuttle's cockpit during his absence. He was also apprised of who the two engineers are that stood in for Tony and Isaac for the remaining test trips. So far, everything seemed to be under control and going well. In the next few months, astronauts would take the shuttle on a full ride into space.

After leaving the supervisor's office, Reggie made his way to his own office. On the way there, he stopped by the break room to grab a snack from the vending machine. As he neared the break room, he heard a loud commotion coming from inside. To his surprise, Russell and Frank were in a heated discussion.

"Hey, is everything okay?" Reggie asked attempting to bring calm to the ever-rising storm.

"No, everything is not okay!" Frank retorted.

"Everything is fine," Russell disagreed.

"Look, I'm not trying to get involved in your personal business, but from my understanding this beef between you two has been going on for some time, and if it continues, it could affect your jobs. Is that what both of you want?"

"I'm tired of dealing with this jerk. He thinks he can treat people anyway he wants to and not suffer the consequences," Frank said steaming with anger.

Reggie wasn't sure if there was a threat embedded in Frank's statement, but if there were, Russell would have to deal with that. It wasn't Reggie's problem to be concerned with. Glancing over at Russell, Reggie didn't see one ounce of concern. Russell was very calm and collected. He gave the impression that this whole ordeal was just child's play. He didn't appear to be taking any of it seriously.

"I'm not sure what you mean, but isn't there some way to leave your personal business out of the workplace?" Reggie asked trying to get Frank to see the bigger picture. Reggie could really care less about who was sleeping with whose wife. He thought they should be more concerned about jeopardizing their careers. Russell stood quietly. He wasn't offering any information, but Frank was feeling free to share what Russell was up to. He was airing all the dirty laundry.

"After Stephanie and Russell decided to get together after Russell left his wife, there wasn't much I could do if my wife wanted to be with him. But now, she's coming back crying to me because he decided he doesn't want her after all. He's been too busy chasing other skirts around here," Frank shared.

"Well, like I said, Frank, I am not trying to get into anyone's business. But, let me give you a word of advice. If Stephanie left you to carry on with Russell, don't you think it's her responsibility to deal with whatever comes with the territory? Why are you trying to fight the battle for a cheating wife?"

"Yeah, I guess you are right. She made her bed, so she has to deal with whatever comes her way."

"So, why are you trying to protect someone who didn't care about how you felt when she made her decision to run after another man?"

"I don't know. I guess because I love her. After all, she is my wife, and we have a son together."

"I understand. But, I still think it's best to leave your personal business out of the workplace. This is really going overboard. Why don't both of you return to your work spaces?"

"Yeah, I will. I'll be leaving for good at the end of this week anyway to return back to New York. He won't have to worry about what I'm doing with Stephanie or anyone else for that matter," Russell said as he walked out.

Frank just stood there looking defeated. He looked mad enough to kill, but he didn't say anything. He looked as if he wanted Reggie to continue counseling him, but Reggie turned away. He continued on his mission to get his snack. Frank sat down at one of the tables and just looked into his hands. He couldn't imagine how everything in his life had gone wrong with coming to California to work on the new space shuttle.

After Reggie purchased his snack, he headed toward the door. Looking back over his shoulder, he said, "I'll see you around. Hope everything works out for you."

"Thanks," Frank said in almost a whisper.

17

After returning to work, Teri found it easy to get back into the swing of things. Her co-workers and her one remaining hospital-bound patient were happy to see her. She had the two receptionists call her other patients, who needed follow up exams, to come in during the week. She was looking forward to reviewing their charts and checking on their prognosis. She was really feeling like her old self in a matter of a day's work, except for her growing belly.

On Friday, her third day of work, Teri received a page on the hospital's intercom system. "Dr. Teri Langston to Surgery Room 4." A patient who was scheduled for surgery was about to be prepped, but the surgeon who was scheduled had not yet arrived to the hospital. Teri was needed to fill in. Hearing the page, Teri immediately grew nervous. When she arrived at Surgery Room 4, Melvin was there waiting for her. When she saw him, she began to calm down.

"Dr. Brown, how are you?" Teri said in a very professional tone.

"I'm doing well, Dr. Langston. It is good to have you back. Now couldn't have been a more perfect time," Melvin said with a hopeful look on his face.

"Why is that?"

"We have a patient here who has been scheduled for surgery today; however, the attending physician is not available. So, to cut to the chase, we need you to fill in."

"Can't you postpone the surgery until the surgeon is available?" Teri may have been feeling great being back in the hospital, but she wasn't sure if she was ready to perform surgery again.

"Actually, we would ordinarily do that, as you know, because the doctor has already familiarized himself with the x-rays and other medical concerns. However, the surgery has already been postponed once. We, along with the patient, are ready to move forward."

For a moment, there was silence in the air. Teri didn't know what to say. Her coming back to work was not a direct indication that she was ready to be in the operating room again. She thought she would be able to slowly return to the surgical room. She knew there were other surgeons available where she wouldn't necessarily need to be used.

"Dr. Langston?" Melvin prodded, as he awaited her consent. From the look on her face, he wasn't sure if she would consent or not. Teri stood there with her arms folded, one hand on her chin and her forefinger resting against her temple. She was pondering the situation. Finally, she lifted her head and looked Melvin directly in his eyes.

"Uh yeah, I'll fill in," Teri slowly agreed.

Melvin immediately turned around to the nursing staff, which was patiently waiting to move ahead, and said, "Prepare the patient." Then, looking back at Teri, he said, "You can do this. You have nothing to worry about. You have removed several aneurysms in the past." Teri didn't reply. She nodded her head and walked towards the sterilization room. As she made her way, she began to wonder who the attendant would be. Before the thought cleared her brainwaves, her question was answered. It was none other than Robbie Showman. *Oh, great*, she thought.

When Robbie saw Teri approaching, he became overfriendly and began apologizing about his testimony in court. "Dr. Langston, it's so good to see you. I heard you were back. How are you? Oh, I see you are having a baby. How are you coming along? Dr. Langston, can you ever forgive me for the things I said in court? I just told it how I saw it. I wasn't trying to say you hurt the little girl. I'm sorry…"

Teri immediately put an end to his discourse. "Robbie, please. I do not have time for small talk. I need to prep for surgery."

"Right, Dr. Langston. I'm sorry. I just wanted you to know…"

"Robbie, please. Be quiet."

"Okay."

Once Teri was fully sanitized and the patient was prepped, Teri quickly reviewed the patient's x-rays to determine the location of the aneurysm. Once located, she gave the instructions for the nurse to shave that part of the patient's scalp. While she watched the shaving, Teri felt her nerves once again begin to move about in her stomach. She took a deep breath, lifted the scalpel, and began the surgery.

A few hours later, Teri successfully completed the surgery. She immediately returned to the sanitation room to clean up. Afterward, she went to the doctors' lounge to grab her white jacket, so she could meet with the patient's family and inform them of the patient's prognosis and the outcome of the surgery.

After sharing the good news regarding the success of the surgery with the family, Teri made her way to the elevator. As soon as she stepped onto the elevator, she felt the baby move. That brought a smile to her face. She couldn't wait to give birth and welcome her baby to the family. But, she had four and a half more months to go.

When the elevator arrived to her destination, Teri felt very comfortable with the decision she had made in the last hour although she had not considered it before going into surgery. Having to perform surgery and experiencing the uneasiness let her know a change needed to be made immediately. She just needed to share her decision with Dr. Brown. Walking up to Dr. Brown's office, she greeted his executive secretary.

"Good afternoon, Melanie. I'm sorry I didn't schedule an appointment, but is Dr. Brown available?"

"He is actually getting ready to leave for lunch. Can you come back in an hour or so?"

"Actually, I will be leaving for the day. Maybe, I'll just call him later."

"Okay, I will let him know to expect your call."

"Thank you."

Just as Teri turned to head back to the elevator, Melvin exited his office. "Ter..., Uh Dr. Langston," Melvin called out as he saw the back of Teri as she was walking away.

"Dr. Brown, I was just stopping by to see you for a quick minute. But, I understand you are on your way to lunch," Teri said hoping he would invite her into his office.

"Oh, it's no problem. I can spare a few minutes."

"Are you sure? I don't want to inconvenience you."

"It's no problem at all. Come on in. How did the surgery go?" Melvin asked as they walked into his office.

"It went well. No problems."

"Great. I didn't have any worries that you could handle it. You must have that same confidence in yourself. But, I'm sure you didn't come in here for a lecture. What's on your mind?"

"I don't think I'm actually ready to be back at work."

"What do you mean? You just performed surgery, and you said it went well."

"I know, but I was so apprehensive. And I was emotionally fatigued. I do not want to place anyone's life in jeopardy."

"It sounds as though you have lost some of your confidence."

"I didn't think I had, but after today, maybe it's true. I think I need just a little more time to get back into the swing of things."

"Okay. I certainly understand. How much time do you think you need? I certainly don't want to rush you. It may do more harm than good."

"I think I should stay off until after the birth of the baby."

"That's quite a while. When are you due?"

"In August."

"Like I said, that's quite a while."

"Well, it's not as long as it sounds. Remember, I was scheduled to take off a month before the baby's birth anyway. So actually, I am only leaving a few months earlier." After adding up the time of her impending absence from work, Teri realized she would be gone a total of six months. "Yeah, I guess that is a long time, but I think it will be better for me, the baby and the patients."

"Well, why don't you give it some more thought and give me a call in a few days."

"Thank you. I will. Let me give it more thought over the weekend, and I will call you on Monday."

"Very well. Tell Reggie I said hello, and we'll see you guys soon."

"I will give him the message. Oh, and don't forget we are going to finish our card tournament. And next time we will switch up the teams. It will be me and Trina against you and Reg."

"Oh, okay. That should be fun. We will have to place a friendly wager on that one."

"As long as you are ready to lose everything, I'm game."

"Oh, I see you have jokes, doc. Hey, take it easy. I'm going to grab a bite to eat and get back to the grind. I have a feeling I have to get some replacements lined up for my best brain surgeon."

18

On her drive home, Teri thought about her husband's response to her taking time off until after the baby is born. She believed he would support her 100%. She felt good about her decision and had peace within her spirit. Her mind left that topic, and she began to focus on food. These days, her mind seemed to focus on food often. The baby had really changed her eating habits. Sometimes she ate often, while at other times she didn't eat enough. All in all, she figured it balanced out.

Still trying to decide what to cook for dinner, Teri turned down her street without having stopped at the grocery store. She didn't know what she really had a taste for. When she pulled up, she automatically pressed the garage door opener. To her surprise, there was a strange car parked in her driveway. She had no idea who the car belonged to, and she wasn't expecting guests. *Maybe Reggie is here and has a guest*, she thought.

After pulling past the car into the garage, she did not see Reggie's car. *Well, if he isn't here, whose car is that?* she questioned in her mind. Just as she reached her hand up to push the button on the remote again, Parker walked around from the front porch inside the garage. He startled her with his unexpected presence.

"Parker! What are you doing?" Teri screamed out to her brother.

Teri's response caused Parker to burst into laughter. "Sorry, sis. I didn't mean to scare you."

"Well, you did. What are you doing here, trying to make me go into premature labor?"

Seeing his sister's stomach bulging, Parker reached over and rubbed her stomach. "No, sis. I need to talk to you," he said with all seriousness.

"What's wrong, hon?"

"Can we go inside?"

"Sure, come on. How's the family?"

"Well, that's what I want to talk to you about."

"Uh-oh, that doesn't sound good."

"No, I don't think it is."

After Teri put her things away and prepared warm drinks for her brother and herself, she could feel the pain emanating from her only sibling. In the thirty-three years that they had known each other, she had never seen him in such a condition. She could not begin to imagine what could be wrong. Being a little selfish and not wanting to hear any bad news at the moment, she started not to even ask. But he had said he had come to talk. So, she would give him the honor of listening to whatever he had to say.

"So, honey," she began, "what's going on?"

"I was served with divorce papers this morning."

"Oh, my goodness, Parker. I am sorry to hear that. Was this unexpected?"

"Well Noel mentioned not long ago that she wanted a divorce, but I really didn't think she would go through with it."

"Well what brought you guys to this point? What's going on?"

"Noel has been seeing someone else, and she says she's in love with him."

"How long has this been going on?"

"I really don't know, but I found out a few months ago. According to her it's been going on for about six months."

"Did you suspect anything?"

"You know I asked myself that same question. I think I just really didn't want to believe that she would do something like that to me, to us, to our family."

"Where did she meet this guy?"

"At work."

"Oh, so it's one of those office flings."

"Again, according to her, it is not a flung. She says they are in love."

"So, Parker, do you still love Noel?"

"Yes, of course. I love her dearly."

"So, what are you going to do? Are you going to let her walk away or are you going to put up a fight?"

"I don't want to let her go, but I don't want to push her away by trying to convince her to stay."

While Teri and Parker were deeply engrossed in their conversation, Reggie walked into the house. He quickly observed the atmosphere and noticed there was a little tension in the air.

"Is everything okay?"

Teri looked at her brother, waiting for him to answer. She didn't want to share his personal business without his consent.

"Not really. Having marital problems," Parker answered.

"I'm sorry to hear that. Is there anything I can do to help?"

"Well, I came over here to get some sisterly advice, but I will take all the help I can get."

"How do you think I can help, hon?" Teri asked.

"Well, I figured you can give me a woman's perspective, plus I remember when you broke up with Pierre before you married Reggie. Pierre really loved you, but you didn't share the same feelings. He kept pursuing you, but to no avail. I'm curious to know what makes a person want to stay with another person and what make them want to go."

"The situation with me and Pierre is much different from yours and Noel's. Pierre and I were two different peas from two different pods. We were going in two different directions in life. That's not to say that people from different backgrounds or different goals can't work together. But we learned we didn't have any commonalities. So, when he continued to pursue me, I felt it was best to move on. But, you and Noel have a foundation and you have three children together."

The three of them talked and shared their perspectives on marriage, divorce, and staying together. The longer they talked, the more they began to get to the root of the problem. Noel was very spoiled, and she loved having all the attention on her. When Parker had decided to return to school for his law degree, Noel slowly began to drift away as Parker became engrossed in his studies. Obviously, she began to get attention from a different source, the guy at work, and she let it envelope her. Now, six months later, she had filed for divorce.

"I think what I will do is suggest a separation rather than a divorce and allow us some time away from each other where she can have a moment to think. Maybe time is what we need. In the end, she will either come back or move on," Parker stated.

19

Over the weekend, Teri shared her feelings with Reggie, her experience with the last surgery, and her desire to take time off. He encouraged her to go with her heart. He wanted what was best for her and their baby. So, the decision was final. Teri would take the next four months off and relax until the baby was born. After the baby's birth, she would take off another two months for her official maternity leave. So, all together she would have six months of rest and relaxation. During that time, she could re-build her confidence in conducting surgeries and prepare the nursery.

On Monday morning, she phoned Melvin's office to make an appointment with him to discuss her final decision about taking off work for the duration of the pregnancy.

"Good morning, Dr. Melvin Brown's office," Melanie answered in a bright and cheery voice.

"Good morning, Melanie. This is Dr. Teri Langston. I would like to schedule an appointment today with Dr. Brown."

"What time would you like to come in?"

"Well, I have another appointment at the hospital at 1:00, so any time before or after if you have it available."

"Okay, he is scheduled to take an early lunch at 11:30, so can you can come in at 12:30? Will that be enough time for your 1:00 appointment?"

"Yes, that will work fine, Melanie. Thank you."

In the few hours Teri had to spare before her hospital appointments, she stopped by her mother's house to see her niece and nephew. Her oldest nephew was in school. Teri loved children, and she spent as much time with her niece and nephews as she could. And, she spoiled them rotten. Every time she stopped in to see them, she tried to take them something, even if it was just a bag of potato chips and a bottle of apple juice. Most of the time though, it was something more tangible like a Barbie doll for her niece or a Tonka truck for her nephews.

Today, she decided to get them something a bit more educational. She took them a set of jigsaw puzzles: one with the full alphabet and the other with numbers 1-10. She knew they would be going to school soon, and she wanted to make sure they were educationally prepared.

When Teri made it to the hospital later that afternoon, she headed directly to the elevator to go up to Melvin's office before her appointment with Dr. Idris. As she waited for the elevator door to open, she heard a loud commotion coming from down the hall. Curious, she stepped back to see what the excitement was. There was a large crowd gathered around something or someone. Teri wanted to see what was going on, so she walked over to take a closer look.

In the center of the crowd was Jessica Chavez. To Teri's surprise, Jessica was walking. She was walking very slowly and a little wobbly, but nonetheless, she was walking. Teri began to scream with joy right along with everyone else. She couldn't believe her eyes. Her prayers for Jessica had been answered. Jessica was smiling as she took small steps while holding her physical therapist's hand. When she lifted her head, she saw Teri.

"Dr. Langston, hi!" Jessica said, who was now nearly four years old.

Everyone's attention was then shifted to Teri. They all began to clap and congratulate both Jessica and Teri. Teri just stood there in awe, as she waved at Jessica. She didn't know what to say. She had mixed emotions. Not long ago, she was getting evil stares from various persons around the hospital. Today, though, she was getting cheers and accolades. She was excited for Jessica, but she didn't know how to receive the cheers. She thought it best to leave. With tears in her eyes, she walked back to the elevator. Once again, she pushed the button to go up.

Just as she stepped inside the elevator, she felt a tug on her arm. Looking behind her, she saw Mrs. Maria Chavez, Jessica's mother and Jessica's brother Javier.

"Yes?" Teri asked.

"Gracias," Maria said with tears in her own eyes.

"You're welcome," Teri said anxious to move on.

Maria and her son Javier began speaking in Spanish to each other. Teri just stood there looking lost, wondering what was going on.

"My mother says she is sorry about the lawsuit. She just did what she was advised to do," Javier said to Teri.

"Tell her it's okay. You guys have a good day," Teri said with her anxiety growing. Javier could tell Teri didn't want to be bothered, so he pulled his mother back. Maria and Javier got off the elevator, and Teri went on up to see Dr. Brown.

After her brief meeting with Melvin, where she shared the good news about Jessica and her decision to take some time off,

Teri made her way to Dr. Idris' office.

"Good afternoon, Sheila. I am here for my 1:00 appointment."

"Okay, Dr. Langston. Dr. Idris is out today, but Dr. Phillips will be filling in," Sheila advised.

"Oh, I wasn't aware of that."

"Yes, an emergency occurred yesterday, and Dr. Idris had to leave town, but she didn't want to cancel her appointments, especially yours."

"Why especially mine?"

"She said it is important for you to have your cervix checked."

"Oh, okay," Teri said uneasily. She really didn't like different doctors fiddling around with her. When she found one she was comfortable with, she stuck with that one until there was some reason for her to change to another one.

"You can go on in to Room 3, and Dr. Phillips will be right in with the attending nurse. Be sure to remove all clothing from the waist down and cover yourself with the gown that's on the table."

Teri went into Room 3 and did exactly what she was instructed. As she waited for the doctor, she thought about Jessica and sent a text to Reggie and her mother to tell them the awesome news. Before long, there was a knock at the door.

"Come in," Teri responded. Dr. Phillips walked in with a nurse trailing behind him. As he introduced himself, Teri sat quietly. She was surprised to learn Dr. Phillips is male. She has always preferred a female doctor. *This is not good*, Teri told herself, as she grew more and more uncomfortable. After explaining the procedure to her, Dr. Phillips asked Teri to lie back on the table. She did as she was told, but she felt her body stiffen.

"Please relax, Dr. Langston. I will be gentle. I promise. You are going to feel my gloved hand on your calf." As he placed his hand on her calf, he asked, "Are you okay?"

"Yes, I'm fine."

"Okay, now my hand will move to your knee, now on your thigh. Just relax."

Teri held her breath as she felt Dr. Phillips' fingers enter into her vaginal cavity, while his other hand pressed on the outside of her stomach. For the next few moments, he performed the exam, and she held her breath the entire time.

"Everything looks good, Dr. Langston. You can get dressed now."

"Thank you, Dr. Phillips."

As Teri got dressed, she continued to feel uneasy. It wasn't anything Dr. Phillips had done. It was an incident that she experienced when she was eleven that left a bad taste in her mouth and a distrust for men. As Teri reflected on the past, she recalled the incident.

One night when Teri was eleven years old, she was taking a bath, and all of a sudden, the bathroom door opened. She was surprised, to say the least. No one had ever walked into the bathroom before when she was bathing, not even her mother. When she looked up to see who was there, to her misfortune, it was her stepfather. She didn't say a word, but he had plenty to say. He walked over to her and told her he was going to show her how to kiss. He instructed her to place her small arms around his neck, and he proceeded to French kiss her. At the same time, he lifted one of her legs out of the tub and placed it on the side of the tub, so she would have one leg up while the other was down. Then, he attempted to insert a finger into her eleven-year-old vagina. At his touch, she dropped her arms from his neck and moved away. She was horrified.

The next night, he came into her room and tried to lift her gown, she kicked and yelled, "No, Daddy! No! I'm sleeping!" At the sound of Teri's voice, her mother called out from the master bedroom and halted him in his tracks. He quietly closed Teri's bedroom door and went back to his own bed with Teri's mother.

All the incidents Teri experienced as a young child caused her to have a great distrust for men. She believed the only thing they wanted was her body. They were not interested in her, her mind, or her abilities. They just wanted sex. These thoughts had led her to stay clear of men while she was growing up, so she would not be victimized.

20

When Teri returned home after her OB/GYN appointment, all she wanted to do was lie down. Just as she headed upstairs to her bedroom, her cell phone rang. It was her mother.

"Hey, Mom."

"Well, hello dear. How are you?"

"I'm doing okay."

"You don't really sound okay. Did you have a bad day?"

"No, not really."

"I'm not sure what that means, but I thought you would be in a good mood with the news of Jessica's recovery and all."

Teri's mind had wandered so far back into her past that she nearly forgot about the events of the day.

"I am," Teri said.

"Teri, you know you can talk to me about anything, don't you?'

"Yes, Mom. I do."

"Well, I'm here if you want to talk. I don't want to pry, and I'm not going to push."

With Priscilla's tender words and show of genuine concern for her daughter's well-being, Teri began to cry. This caused even more concern within Priscilla.

"Teri, do you need me to come over there?"

"No, Mom."

"Is it the baby?"

"No, the baby is fine."

"Well, what is it?"

Teri explained to her mother what happened during her prenatal appointment and the flashbacks the exam brought on. She described how the exam made her feel and her constant suspicions about men's intentions. She didn't suspect Dr. Phillips personally, but she sure didn't want him examining her either. As she explained all of this to her mother, she began to feel alone and as though there was no one who could really understand what she was going through and how she felt.

"Teri, I'm so sorry you experienced that. We have talked about this time and time again. I don't know how else to help you to move beyond the past except by telling you to go to see a therapist. I know in the past you said you didn't want to see one or air your private life with a complete stranger. But, maybe you will reconsider. Sweetheart, you want to be sure you are physically, financially, and emotionally healthy when your baby is born. I'm sure the financial and physical parts are well taken care of, but remember the emotional part of you is just as important, if not more."

Just as Priscilla completed her statement, her other line rang. "Teri, hold on a minute. That's Parker calling."

As Teri held on, she thought about all her mother had just said and the advice she had given Teri in the past. Deep down Teri knew she needed to do something different to attempt to diffuse the bomb that was growing and ticking inside of her. However, she didn't know if she could honestly say she was ready for therapy.

When her mother returned back to the phone, she sounded exhausted. Now, it was Teri's turn to worry about her.

"Mom, why do you sound so out of breath?"

"I was just praying for Parker. Right now, I'm just praying for both my children. When you two hurt, I hurt as well."

"We know, Mom. What's going on with Parker? Is it him and Noel again?'

"Again? Don't you mean 'still'?"

"Yeah, I guess. What do you think will happen with them?"

"Teri, you know I don't like to speculate. I just pray that he allows the Lord to lead him."

"Amen to that!" Teri agreed.

"I asked Parker to come to dinner tomorrow, so we can talk in person. Why don't you and Reggie come too?"

"Let me check Reggie's schedule, and I will let you know if he can make it. Because I am officially on maternity leave/vacation, I will be there. What time?"

"How about 6:00?"

"Sounds good. Should I bring something?"

"No, not this time. With all you guys do for me, I don't need a thing."

Teri and Parker take great care of their mother. They had paid her house off, and each month, they gave her a monthly allowance. She collected her social security retirement, but there wasn't much left after she paid her bills and bought groceries for the month. So, her children took the responsibility of her bills, and she was able to keep her entire check each month to do whatever she wanted to do. When each of them gets a raise on their jobs, they increase the amount they give to her.

At first, Priscilla put up a fight when they told her what they wanted to do for her. They explained to her that she didn't need to keep paying a mortgage each month when there was only less than twenty thousand dollars left to pay. They finally convinced her to let them pay it off. She vowed she would pay them back. They said they would not hear of it after all she had done for them throughout their whole lives.

After passing through that hurdle, they snuck around her house and located all her bills. Each month, they paid them without even asking her. Each time Priscilla received a bill, it showed a credit instead of an amount due. She finally caught on to them and decided to not put up a fight.

Then, they got her bank account number and began to deposit $250 each in it each month, giving her an extra $500 on top of her social security to live with, vacation with, or save. The choice was hers. Any repairs she needed around the house, they took care of them. Every five years, they made sure she had a new car to drive. It was her choice. They helped her get whatever she wanted. Plain and simple, Priscilla was spoiled. She was well taken care of. That was just Parker and Teri's way of showing their mother how much they love her.

After speaking with her mother and knowing she would see both her mother and brother the next day, Teri felt a little better. She even had a little energy. After hanging up with her mother, Teri took a nice long hot, soothing shower. The hot water put her in a meditative mood.

When she turned off the shower, a muscular, well-sculpted arm handed her a towel. "Thanks, honey," Teri said joyfully. She was happy to know that her husband had made it in early from work.

After drying off, Teri stepped out of the shower. Her husband was waiting with open arms. "How did your appointments with Melvin and Sharon go today?" Reggie asked as he caressed her nude belly.

"The appointment with Melvin went well. Of course, he didn't want me to take off so early before the baby is due, but he certainly understands. And, my second appointment ended up being with Dr. Phillips and not Sharon. She had an emergency and Dr. Phillips stood in for her."

"Ok, is everything okay with the baby?"

"Yes, both the baby and I are doing fine," Teri said softly.

"Babe, what's wrong?" Reggie asked, detecting a little uneasiness in his wife's voice.

"Dr. Phillips is a man," she said staring at Reggie.

"Oh, I see. Are you okay?"

"Physically, I'm fine. But, I must say, with him doing the exam, I felt creepy."

"I can imagine. Is there anything I can do to make you feel better?"

"No, I'm just going to lie down. The feeling will wear off soon," she said anxious to get away from his hands that had left her belly and had begun to explore other parts of her body. She loved her husband's touch, but at times, she just didn't want to be touched at all.

21

The next day, Teri left home anxious to see her mother and brother. Before going directly to her mother's home, she decided to stop by the florist to pick up a beautiful flower arrangement. As she looked around for the perfect arrangement, one that was very colorful and one that would lighten the atmosphere in the house, she saw another customer who seemed to be in search of the perfect arrangement also. From the looks of things, he seemed to be deep in thought. He was standing in the refrigerated section looking at the beautiful arrangements of red roses.

"You must be looking for flowers for someone special," she observed.

"Yes, she is very special to me," the man said with a smile on his face.

"Is it a special occasion?" Teri asked, hoping she wasn't overstepping her bounds.

"Yes, first date."

Teri stopped and looked at the man with a questioning look. Her look asked, "Why would you give a woman a full bouquet of roses on the first date?" She thought that would send a signal of coming on too strong. Her looked provoked laughter within the man.

"Let me explain. The roses are for my daughter. She is seventeen, and she is going on her first date. I want to let her know that no matter what happens tonight, I will always be here for her."

"Oh, that's really sweet and thoughtful. I thought you were going to make your first date your last date," she said laughing. The man laughed with her.

"Yeah, I probably would scare someone off giving them a large bouquet of flowers on our first date. But, you never know, some women like that kind of attention."

"Yeah, but I'm glad they're for your daughter. I hope she has a good time tonight."

"Thank you," the man said as he made his way to the cash register.

Once Teri located the perfect arrangement for her mom, she continued her drive over. She thought about the topics they would discuss over dinner: Parker's marital problems and her own issues with abuse. She had never sat down with her brother and told him everything she had gone through. She had alluded to certain instances in conversation here and there, but they had never come right out and discussed it. She had a feeling he knew some things, but he never asked her, and she never bothered to tell. It was her experience that most men didn't want to face the reality that some of their counterparts were monsters: pedophiles and rapists. They seemed to rather believe it didn't happen in their family.

Pulling up in front of her mother's home, she noticed her brother's car in the driveway. *Let the games begin,* she thought. She walked up to the door and purposefully left the flowers in the back seat. Using her key to let herself in, she found her family in the kitchen.

"Hey, everybody."

"Hey, sis," Parker responded.

"Hi, sweetheart. Where is Reggie?"

"He is working, but he said he will try to come by when he gets off, if we are still here. If not, he wants me to bring him a plate home."

"Okay, well there is plenty. Wow, I see your belly is growing. You look so cute being pregnant," Priscilla said admiring her daughter.

"Thanks, Mom. Hey, hon, can you go get the vase of flowers from my backseat?"

"Sure," Parker said and headed out the front door after he hugged his sister as he walked past her.

"Mom, do you think it will be okay talking about everything in front of Parker?"

"Girl, your brother is over 30 years old. I am sure he knows plenty about what goes on in the world."

"I'm sure he does, but he doesn't know about me."

"I think it will be okay, Teri," her mother assured her.

At that moment, Parker walked back in with the flowers and placed them on the dining room table. "What will be okay?" he asked.

"Oh, the flowers are beautiful, Teri. Thank you. Will it be okay for them to be in here with us?" Priscilla asked totally ignoring her son's question as she and Teri continued to set the table. For a quick moment, Teri had to recall what Priscilla was referring to.

"Oh, yeah. It's fine. I haven't had a problem with flowers for the last couple of months. I had forgotten about that."

"About what?" Parker asked feeling totally out of the loop.

"When I first got pregnant, I couldn't eat a lot of foods or deal with certain smells, flowers being one of them. But, it's a lot better now."

"I remember Noel going through that too. But, you know- it was different with every child," Parker said with sadness in his eyes.

"So, what has happened since we last spoke about Noel filing divorce papers? Did you sign them?" Teri asked as they sat down to eat.

"No, I didn't sign them. I asked Noel if we could sit and talk, just the two of us. She agreed, and we went out to dinner. I told her where I stood with us. I let her know she and our children are the most important people to me, and I am not willing to walk away without giving it my best effort. I also told her she was not leaving with the kids. If she wants to go and explore, she can, but the kids will not be going for the ride."

"What did she say to that?"

"I actually believe she was relieved. She didn't put up a fight about the kids at all."

"So, what does all of this mean?" Priscilla asked, in between bites of steak with Beef Bourguignon sauce.

"By the end of the night," Parker continued, "we had decided to not move forward with the divorce but to have a trial separation instead."

"For how long?" Teri inquired.

"Three months."

"So, who's going to be moving out?" Priscilla asked.

"Actually, she already has. I told her because she wants the separation or divorce, she could leave. The kids and I are staying in our own home and in our own beds."

"So, how do you feel overall, hon?" Teri asked.

"I feel better than I did when I received the divorce papers. Divorce is so final. I don't know what will happen, but at least, we are giving ourselves an opportunity to have some breathing room to think things over."

With that final comment about Parker's situation, they all began to dig in to the savory meal Priscilla had spent the last few hours preparing. The two siblings missed their mother's cooking. Halfway through the meal, Priscilla said, "Sweetheart, have you thought about my suggestion?"

"I thought about it," Teri said nonchalantly.

"Thought about what?" Parker asked.

"I suggested your sister go to therapy," Priscilla answered.

"What do you need therapy for, sis? Is the trial still bothering you?"

"No, it's not that. Oh, I didn't tell you. Yesterday, Jessica was walking."

"That's excellent news! So, if it's not the trial what is it?"

Very calmly, Teri began to fill her brother in on some of the incidents she experienced as a child and the effects they had on her. She didn't want to overwhelm him with too much detail, so she shared just enough for him to understand the issue was seriously overwhelming her life even twenty plus years later.

As Parker listened to Teri, tears began to well up in his eyes as he heard how his sister had been violated. Finally, he excused himself from the table. He felt as though he had a dagger in his heart. He felt helpless that he couldn't fix her problems.

After Parker left the room, Teri looked at her mother as if to ask, *What now?* Priscilla returned a reassuring look to let Teri know that she and her brother would both be okay.

"Teri Lynn, I want you to take my suggestion seriously."

"I am, Mom. I am giving it serious thought."

Parker walked back into the room, grabbed his sister and hugged her tightly. "It will be okay, sis. I am here for you." Teri breathed a sigh of relief knowing she could move forward with her healing.

22

Nearly a month later, Teri was scheduled to visit Dr. Idris for her sixth-month prenatal checkup. The pregnancy was progressing well, and Teri was experiencing more movement from the baby. During her appointment, she would learn the sex of her baby. Reggie wanted it to be a surprise, but Teri was ready to go shopping and put the nursery together. She wanted to know if she should get a white or cherry wood crib. She wanted to know what color to have the walls painted and what types of decorations to put up. She wasn't too thrilled about the use of yellows and greens to make everything unisex. She wanted either a girl's nursery or a boy's nursery. With her multiple explanations, Reggie finally agreed it would be okay for her to tell him the sex of the baby when she found out.

As Teri sat on the table waiting for Sharon to come into the examination room, she recalled the last time she was there. While Teri was deep in thought, Sharon knocked lightly on the door and entered. Noticing her friend's demeanor, Sharon asked, "What is it, Teri? You look to be a million miles away."

"Hi, Sharon. I was just thinking about my last exam."

"Was there a problem with Dr. Phillips?"

"Oh, no. It wasn't him," Teri said quickly to dispel any problems before they began.

"Well what then?" Sharon prodded. Teri began to freely share about her experiences, her apprehensions, and the effects. She shared and shared and shared, as tears fell from her eyes. Sharon pulled up a stool and quietly listened. When Teri was done, Sharon reached over, grabbed her hand, and began to console her. "I know how you feel," Sharon said as she wiped her own tears away. "When I was seven years old," she continued, "my uncle began raping me. This continued until I was eleven years old."

"Oh, my God," Teri exclaimed. "I had no idea."

"Yes, I know, just as I had no idea about you. Abuse is not something people generally wear on the outside of them. It is not something people broadcast. And, like stress, it can be a silent killer. It will eat you alive if you allow it to and fail to get the tormenting spirits under control."

"What do you mean?"

"Scars from abuse have ruined relationships between families, in marriages, and even in work relationships. Everything must be brought to the surface and discussed. It cannot be allowed to lie dormant and fester. It will spread like a cancer and do great harm."

"Wow, Sharon, you have really given this some thought," Teri said. She was really impressed with the responses and advice she was receiving from her friend. It wasn't the everyday run of the mill responses that people usually throw at you to get you to be quiet or go away because they really don't care about your problems.

"Yes, I have. I dealt with it for too long, and it is what ultimately led to my divorce when I was married to my first husband. My husband didn't understand me, nor did he really try.

People act is if though abuse is something like an old garment that a person can shed and throw in the trash, but it isn't that easy. It doesn't work that way. The scars of abuse are similar to those of a third or fourth degree burn. They become part of you. Over time, they may fade as new skin grows and the old skin sheds, but they never completely go away."

"Having gone through what you went through, you sound really strong, Sharon. What did you do to get to this point?"

"I started going to therapy. Now, I am one of the counselors."

"How long were you in therapy?"

"About three years."

"Wow, that's a long time."

"Well, the scars were deep. And, not only did those three years help me, but the counseling that I'm doing with others helps me too."

"I can imagine that it does. That's awesome."

"Yes, therapy can work wonders for the soul, but a person has to commit to it and not expect miracles overnight. But, we can talk about all of this more a little later. Let me do your exam and the ultrasound, so I can see if I'm going to have a niece or a nephew, plus I have other patients waiting, my dear."

"Yes, I'm ready to find out. Thank you for sharing with me, Sharon."

"It's my pleasure. I hope I was of help."

"Yes, I actually feel a little better after our brief counseling session," Teri said with smile as she lay back on the examination table.

Dr. Idris quickly moved from friend mode into gynecologist mode. She had one of the nurses hook Teri up to the fetal monitor and the ultrasound machine. In minutes, Teri could hear the baby's heart beat and see the movements. She had felt life inside of her, but now she had an opportunity to see life inside of her. Hearing her baby's heartbeat was breathtaking.

As Teri looked at the ultrasound, she kept wondering, *Boy or girl? Girl or boy?* Sharon saw Teri looking intently at the machine, but she just let her look. She kept her eyes peeled on the paperwork she was filling in.

"So?" Teri asked.

"So what?" Sharon answered as she continued looking down.

"Are you going to tell me the sex?"

"Oh, you want to know the sex?"

"Yes, of course. We talked about this at my last visit. Remember?"

"Um, no. I don't think so."

"Sure you do. And, you just brought it up a few minutes ago. Are you stalling on purpose?"

"I'm not sure what you mean," Sharon said with a straight face as she looked at Teri over her eyeglasses.

"Sharon, come on!" Teri yelled.

"Um ma'am, please don't disturb my other patients."

"Sharon, if you don't stop stalling, you won't have any other patients because I'm going to start screaming bloody murder."

Sharon burst out laughing. She couldn't keep her composure any longer. There was nothing like teasing an expecting mother when she wanted to know the sex of her unborn child. They all became very antsy and demanding. Sharon loved giving them a run for their money. But, time was getting short and she really did have other patients to see, so her time of torturing Teri had to come to an end.

"Well, my dear. You are going to have a beautiful bouncing bundle of joy."

"Uh huh," Teri said, still waiting.

"You are going to have a beautiful daughter," Sharon said with a wide grin.

"Oh, wow!" Teri screamed.

The news brought joy to her heart. She had always wanted a girl around her. She never had a sister, but now she would have a daughter. She grinned from ear to ear. She couldn't wait to share the news with Reggie, Priscilla and Trina. Trina had already scheduled a shopping spree for the next weekend. Now, Teri knew what to shop for.

After leaving the hospital, Teri stopped by *Baby's R Us*. She was ready to go shopping for her baby girl, but she issued a lot of self-restraint. She silently vowed to only pick up a few items. She would save the big shopping spree for Saturday.

As she sauntered around the store in the layette section, she looked at everything from bottles and socks to car seats and high chairs. Occasionally, she would stop and rub her belly. She had waited for this moment for a long time, and it was finally here. She was having a baby with the man she loves and who loves her. They were growing their family.

In the midst of the joy was always the uncertainty of what if they didn't do everything just right. What if they made a mistake that had long-lasting effects on the baby? What if this and what if that? She knew she couldn't let those types of questions plague her mind. So, she quickly dismissed them and went along with her moment of joy.

When Teri returned home, she was very energized. She began preparing dinner for her husband and herself. She pulled out all the stops, no holds barred. While dinner was simmering, she began to set the table. In Reggie's chair, she placed a gift bag. In the bag, there were a few baby items she had picked up when she was at the store. One item was a pink and white bib that read, 'Daddy's Favorite Girl.'

After Reggie arrived home, he kissed his glowing wife, showered quickly and made his way to the table. He was ready to devour the delicious smelling food. When he pulled his chair out, he saw the gift bag. With a smile on his face, he opened the bag and pulled out the pink items. All he could say while smiling was, "Uh oh, I'm going to be outnumbered!"

23

Two months later, the time had finally arrived for the astronauts to take the space shuttle for its first official flight. The engineers had re-tested the machine several times and had placed their stamp of approval on it. The world was waiting to see *NASA*'s latest invention, known as *Forager*. At the same time, however, everyone was nervous after the last incident with the fire and two engineers getting burned. The flight was being televised around the world on the major news channels. Traffic had been drastically minimized in the streets because most people were somewhere glued to a television set or watching the live stream through the internet.

Reggie and some of his *NASA* buddies decided to make an event out of it. They met at a local *Buffalo Wild Wings*. Some engineers and their mates were seated all across the bar area, while other engineers were seated at tables throughout the restaurant. *NASA* had graciously provided the engineers with t-shirts with *Forager* printed across the chest and also made them available for sale. So, some of the engineers' mates were wearing them too. Everyone who came into the restaurant took notice of them. Some even stopped to make light conversation and to ask them about their experience in being involved in the building of the newest space shuttle. The engineers were eating up all the attention, and their mates did not mind it one bit either. It was a happy moment for all.

When the broadcast began, via satellite from Florida, a hush fell over the crowd. In the once noise-filled overcrowded restaurant, you could hear a pin drop. At the beginning of the broadcast, a pre-recorded introduction of the team of engineers was shown. As each engineer was announced on screen, he or she stood up and took a bow in the restaurant. The co-engineers and their mates gave a round of applause. The crowd at *Buffalo Wild Wings* cheered right along with them.

After the engineers were introduced, the astronauts were announced on site. Each astronaut had an opportunity to say a few words about how they felt about being appointed for this new space journey. While speaking, each one of them took the opportunity to say words to his/her family. Through all the joy and excitement of astronauts traveling into space is the reality they may not make it back to Earth.

After the astronauts boarded *Forager*, the door was shut. About fifteen minutes later, *Forager* lifted off. Around the world, cheers could be heard. People in the United States were celebrating because of our continued accomplishments in space. Other nations cheered in celebration with us, knowing if we are successful, they too can be successful when it comes to their space exploits.

At *Buffalo Wild Wings*, after the broadcast ended with *Forager* disappearing into the clouds, everyone settled down to enjoy a meal of seasoned chicken wings and a select choice of sides, along with delectable beverages.

As they were eating, Reggie thought about his wife who had decided to stay home and rest. She had gained a little more weight than she anticipated, and she became fatigued easily. She had asked him to bring her home an order of Parmesan wings and onion rings. He made the order, finished his meal, said his goodbyes, and drove home.

When Reggie arrived home, Teri was on the treadmill. He knew she was self-conscious about her weight, but he didn't mind one bit. She had a sexy glow that he found irresistible.

"Babe, don't overdo the exercise," Reggie said with concern.

"I won't. The exercise is good for the baby and me. Since I haven't been at work and moving around like I used to, my body has become relaxed. I want to start working on this weight now before it gets worse."

"How many pounds have you gained overall, Teri?"

"I'm not sure, but I think it is about thirty-two pounds. Sharon said about 25 pounds is associated with the baby."

"So, the other seven pounds is on you?"

"Yeah."

"And that concerns you? Don't even answer. I can see that it does. But, take it from me. It shouldn't. You look great," Reggie said with a sparkle in his eye. Noticing, how her husband was admiring her, Teri dismounted the treadmill and walked over to him. She loved the attention he gave her.

"You always know the right things to say to put me in the right mood," she said with her arms around his neck. Without another word, Reggie took his wife by the hand, walked across the hall into their bedroom and closed the door. He didn't want this moment to slip by.

24

One week after *Forager* launched into space, Teri's baby shower was held in the Grand Ball Room at the Hyatt Regency Hotel. Trina had made all the arrangements with Priscilla's help. Trina was responsible for getting all friends and coworkers together, while Priscilla was responsible for contacting all family members. The baby shower was co-ed for women and men alike. Of course, not many men showed up, but those who are close to Reggie came in full force.

There were approximately seventy people in attendance. It was the largest baby shower any of them had ever been to. Everyone had been waiting for quite some time for Reggie and Teri to have a baby, so this was a grand occasion. Even Parker came because he was excited to be an uncle for the first time and because his sister always supported him in everything he did. He wanted to return the favor.

At the shower, everyone had a blast. There was so much food that everybody took an extra plate home. There were plenty of games and prizes for everyone to win. The gifts for Teri and Reggie included two strollers, a swing, a car seat, a high chair, a walker, several baby bags, blankets, pillows, dresses, bottles, shoes, socks, stuffed animals, lots of diapers, and everything a little girl needs either when she is first born or sometime during her first year. When Teri and Reggie saw all the items, they smiled to themselves and just shook their heads thinking about all the stuff they had just bought over the last month as they continued to prepare for their daughter's arrival. From the looks of things, they wouldn't need to buy anything for nearly a year, except diapers of course. They felt truly blessed by all the love that was shown towards them and their unborn daughter.

Just as the baby shower was about to wrap up, Reggie decided it would be a great idea for everyone to stand around the room and hold hands. He wanted to pray a blessing over the baby and for a smooth delivery for Teri. Everyone began to stand up and make their way along the walls of the room. That was the only way they could fit into one big circle.

Right at that moment, Noel walked in the door. Not knowing who she was and thought she was returning to the party, someone asked her to join the circle. Parker was so busy making small talk with one of the guests that he did not see his wife walk into the room. Priscilla got his attention and sent him over to Noel.

Parker was surprised to see her. He didn't even know that she knew where he was. He hadn't spoken to her all week. As he approached her, he suddenly began to feel sick to his stomach. Noel had bruises all over her face. When she saw his facial expression, she began to cry. Parker hurried over to her, took her hand, and walked her outside. He did not want their children to see her in that condition.

"Was that Mommy?" Parker Jr. asked.

"Where?" Tania, his little sister, asked.

Priscilla quickly grabbed the children to stand next to her in the circle, so the prayer could commence. Reggie, noticing something was desperately wrong, quickly led the prayer and released everyone to go. After Teri and Reggie said their goodbyes, they quickly went to find Parker and Noel, while Priscilla stayed with the gifts and the children. Trina and Melvin quickly began to pack everything in Teri's and Reggie's cars only to find out everything was not going to fit. At that point, they began loading items into their own car until all gifts were out the banquet hall.

In another part of the hotel, Parker was consoling Noel. Her coworker, the one she had left her husband for, had beaten her once again. Before today, she had not told anyone about the abuse, except for one of her close friends. She was so embarrassed because she had left a good man and settled for someone she didn't even know, only for pure sexual attraction. She had risked twelve years of marriage and her happy family of five for a stranger. Sure, there were some tough moments and moments when she wasn't a hundred percent happy, but it was nothing compared to what she had walked into.

After explaining to Parker what had transpired with her boyfriend, Noel asked him if she could come back home. Although he really wanted her to come back home, he didn't want her to only come because of what happened in her affair. He wanted to know that she really wanted to be back with him and with their children. If he allowed her to come back at that moment, he would always wonder if she only left the other man due to the violence or because she felt she had made a mistake breaking up their marriage.

"Noel, I know you are really in a rough spot, but I don't want you to come back under these circumstances. Maybe I should get you a hotel room."

"You don't have to do that. She can stay at our house," Teri said as she walked up and overheard the last part of their conversation.

"I don't want to impose," Noel said looking down at her hands. She was feeling totally embarrassed; she felt like she had betrayed the entire family.

"It's no imposition at all, Noel. You are family." Teri then turned to Parker and said, "Hon, why don't you let Mom take the kids, so Noel can go to the house and pack some clothes to come to my house."

"I *will* need to do that because I left out of there so fast that I didn't grab anything," Noel said as she began to cry. Parker didn't know whether to console her or let her feel hurt and guilty. Teri detected his ambivalence, so she sat next to Noel and comforted her. Although Teri did not appreciate for one minute the pain Noel had caused her only sibling and their children, she didn't appreciate Noel being hit by a man. She could only imagine the confusion Noel was feeling. Teri did not wish that type of pain on anyone.

After leaving the hotel, Parker and Noel went to their home to pack some of Noel's clothing. Teri and Reggie caravanned to their home, with Melvin and Trina trailing behind them. Once the four friends arrived to Teri and Reggie's home, Trina was all ears. She wanted to know what was going on between Parker and Noel. Once the women were upstairs in the nursery putting some of the new items away, Trina said, "Spill it!" Wanting to make her friend squirm a bit, Teri played dumb.

"Spill what?" she asked.

"I know you think you're cute and all, even in your last month, when you are big enough to pop, but you better stop playing and tell me."

"Girl, tell you what?"

"What's going on between your brother and his wife? Please tell me Parker didn't put his hands on her."

"Girl, please. Of course not. I'm pretty sure her boyfriend did it."

"Her boyfriend? When did they get divorced? Did I miss something?"

"No, they are not divorced. Noel wanted a divorce, but Parker suggested a separation instead."

"Why would she want to divorce Parker with his fine self?"

"She got involved with one of her coworkers and moved in with him."

"I don't understand why women who have a good man always want to leave him for a knucklehead."

"Yeah, tell me about it. Good men are hard to come by. If a woman is fortunate enough to get her hands on one, she should hold onto him."

"Here here," Trina said holding up a baby bottle. Teri found a baby bottle, raised it, and tapped it against the one Trina was holding. They both began to laugh uncontrollably.

"Girl, you are crazy," Teri said.

"Seriously, sis? You are the crazy one," Trina's tone turned serious.

"Why do you say that?" Teri asked, turning her full attention to her friend.

"You are about to allow your cheating sister-in-law to live in your house."

"Yes, I know, but my brother loves her. Also, she is the mother of my niece and nephews. And, I have a feeling they are going to get back together. We all make mistakes, Trina. And at the same time, we all need a support system."

"Yes, Florence Nightingale. You are right of course. I just don't want to see any of you get hurt, especially that fine brother of yours and his cute little kids."

"Thanks for caring. Speaking of kids when are you guys going to have some of your own?" Teri's question caused Trina to suddenly become quiet. "I'm sorry. Did I hit a sore spot?"

"Yes, but it's okay. I can't have children."

"Oh, I'm so sorry."

"It's okay. We came to terms with it a long time ago. I knew my situation even before I married Melvin. He knew from the beginning, and he said he loved me enough to marry me with or without being able to have children."

"That is so sweet. That's the kind of love I'm talking about."

"Well, that's the kind of love you and Reggie have too. Right?"

"Yes, I have really been blessed."

"We both have," Trina said as she and Teri high-fived each other. "Well, sis. I need to run. And I really don't want to be here when 'what's-her-name' gets here. I may have to lay hands on her for being so stupid."

"Yeah, I hear you. Hopefully, she has learned her lesson."

After Melvin and Trina left, Reggie and Teri began to settle in for the night. They were completely worn out from the day's festivities. Because they knew Noel was coming over, they stayed downstairs in the family room until they heard the doorbell ring. Once Noel arrived and was settled into the guest room, Teri and Reggie retired for the night.

Noel, on the other hand, found it difficult to rest. She kept replaying the last year over and over in her mind. She couldn't believe how everything had gone wrong in such a short time frame. One moment, she and Parker were happy and living the American dream and the next moment, they were talking divorce and separation. *This was all my doing*, she thought. *All Parker wanted to do was better himself for his family. Why couldn't I just have had a bit more patience?* With all the thoughts she had running through her mind, all she could do was cry. Finally, she cried herself to sleep.

25

When *Forager* left for the space mission, the intent of the astronauts was to stay in space for nearly one month. In the past, astronauts have stayed in orbit for approximately twenty-eight days. This team of astronauts had planned to do the same. They had enough equipment and supplies to do so. However, one astronaut became ill. This was a mystery to everyone because there are no germs in space. The astronaut must have contracted something that had gone undetected when he was checked by his physician prior to leaving. Each astronaut had to undergo a mandatory physical examination in order to be approved for orbit. In an effort to cover all bases, just in case a virus had set in that had gone undetected, the crew members took medical supplies with them, including cough medicine.

Once the astronaut began to experience cold symptoms, he immediately began to take doses of the cough medicine. However, it was to no avail. He fell ill, and then, a second astronaut became ill as well. When both astronauts failed to recover, the mission was brought to a halt, and the shuttle was returned to Earth only two weeks after it had departed. The landing was made in California, at Edwards Air Force Base, near the city of Lancaster.

When *Forager* touched down, the local *NASA* engineers were there to greet the astronauts and welcome them back to Earth. It was a successful journey and a good cause for a celebration. This time, the engineers and the astronauts were to celebrate together, for all of them had made a great contribution to the history of the United States. Knowing the astronauts were most likely craving home cooking, the engineers opted to take them to *Hometown Buffet*. They would have preferred to go to *Golden Coral* or *Wood Grill*, but neither of those restaurants is in Lancaster.

Just as the engineers and astronauts loaded into the vans *NASA* provided, Reggie received a call. Looking at his caller ID, he saw it was Teri calling. He hoped she was only calling to say hello, but deep down inside, he knew it was time. Sure enough, he heard his wife say these words, "I'm on my way to the hospital. Meet me there." She sounded so calm, but he knew she had to be very scared inside. She had never had a baby before, so she really didn't know what to expect. Neither did he for that matter. Teri's call meant Reggie would be unable to join in the celebration. This was disheartening to him. On the other hand, he was excited to have the opportunity to be there to welcome his new baby girl into the world. So, he immediately said his goodbyes, got into his car, and made the drive from Lancaster to Los Angeles. Teri was due to deliver at the same hospital at which she worked. He prayed he would not miss the delivery. The drive would take him about an hour and a half.

As Reggie was making his way to the hospital as fast as he could without getting a ticket, Teri was also making her way to the hospital. She and Trina had been out having lunch when her water broke. They swung by Teri's house to get her pre-packed overnight bag and then headed to Kaiser.

The contractions were very fierce; Teri had to lean back in the car seat in order to keep herself calm and to try to alleviate some of the excruciating pain. She moaned, and she breathed. Trina attempted to soothe her, but not having had a baby herself, she really didn't know what advice to give her friend.

When Teri arrived to the hospital, an emergency room attendant was awaiting her arrival. Getting her safely into the wheelchair, he whisked her away to the maternity ward, where Dr. Idris had already had a nurse prepare a bed for her.

Safely tucked in bed, Teri was hooked up to the fetal monitor, and her cervix was checked. She had dilated to four centimeters. Dr. Idris could see that her friend/patient was in an extreme amount of pain, so she had one of the attending nurses administer pain medication intravenously. The medicine caused Teri to become sleepy, and eventually, she drifted off into a light sleep.

When Reggie arrived to the maternity ward, he was escorted to Teri's room. He immediately walked over to her bed and placed a soft kiss on her forehead. Feeling her husband's touch, Teri awakened. A smile immediately covered her face. But at the occurrence of a contraction, the smile quickly vanished just as soon as it had come.

For the next hour, Reggie tried to bring comfort to his wife. Priscilla arrived and joined Trina and Reggie. The three of them sat around making small talk.

In an effort to get the latest news on Parker and his wife, Trina asked Priscilla how they were doing.

"Well, Noel went back home to her husband and kids. They are trying to make it work. Although Parker loves her, it is going to be hard for him to get past the fact that she was with another man. You know, men don't deal with infidelity as well as women do. They expect their women to be faithful."

"Mom, I must say you called it right on that one," Reggie agreed, while profusely nodding his head.

"I just hope they can put the past behind them and move on for the sake of their marriage and for the sake of their children. I don't care what anyone says, children really do need both parents in the home."

"I completely agree with you," Trina said. "I was tremendously blessed to have both my mother and father raise me and my sister and brothers."

"Are your parents still together now?" Priscilla asked.

"Yes, they are," Trina said with a smile, as she thought of her loving mother and her devoted father.

"That's good," both Reggie and Priscilla said.

While the three of them talked, Teri fell into a deeper sleep. The medicine was finally working.

As Teri continued to sleep, her brother walked into her hospital room. Their mother had called him to let him know his sister was in labor. After he had settled into his seat, Reggie, Priscilla and Trina began to ask questions about him and his wife. They knew Noel had returned home, but they wanted to get an update on how everything was going between them.

"Well, it is a day-by-day process," Parker began.

"Yes, well we can understand that," his mother offered.

"Do you feel that you can really trust her after what she did?" Reggie asked.

"I actually thought that would be the hardest part, but to tell you the truth, the hard part is wondering whether or not she really wants to be with me. If I can get assurance in that area, I think we will be okay."

"Well, only time can answer that question," Trina said.

"I agree. That is why we have separate bedrooms for now. I don't want to move too quickly to getting things back to where they used to be. I want it to be a natural process."

"I really don't know how you can do it, man. I don't think I could," Reggie said honestly.

"Hopefully, I'm not fooling myself. I'm doing this for our family."

"Everybody makes mistakes here and there. Sometimes, we just need to grow past them," Priscilla said.

"What about the children? How did you guys explain to them the reason Mommy and Daddy aren't sleeping in the same room?" Trina asked.

"Kids are smarter than we give them credit for. When Noel first left, I explained, 'Mommy is going to be living somewhere else for a little while.' When she came back, I told them she was back, but she needed to get a lot of rest, so she would be sleeping downstairs in the guest bedroom. The younger two said, 'Okay,' but I know Parker Jr. knows something more is going on. If he has questions, I will answer them. But so far, he hasn't asked anything else."

In the middle of the conversation, Teri awoke. She looked around at all of their faces and said, "Get the nurse." Reggie was the first one to jump up. He ran into the hallway and over to the nurses' station. The nurse immediately went into Teri's room and began to check the fetal monitor. The baby's heartbeat was elevated. The next step was to check Teri's cervix. The nurse very calmly placed gloves on her hands and asked Trina and Parker to leave the room. Afterward, she quickly checked Teri's cervix and saw she was full dilated. It was time for her to deliver.

26

Teri was disconnected from the fetal monitor, and her bed was rolled down to the delivery room. Reggie and Priscilla followed behind her holding hands, while softly saying a prayer. Trina and Parker stayed behind in the room to wait for the birth of the baby. Finally having a free moment from the time they drove over to the hospital to now, Trina took an opportunity to call her husband to give him an update on Teri's progress.

Following Trina's example, Parker took the opportunity to call Noel and the children to make sure all was well at the house. When Noel did not answer the phone, Parker immediately became nervous. When Parker had left home, Noel stated she and the children would be home making cookies all afternoon. *Where could they be?* he thought. This was his first time leaving Noel alone with the children since she had been back home.

Noticing the perplexed look on Parker's face, Trina asked, "What's wrong, Parker?"

"Oh, I'm just trying to locate Noel and my kids. I called the house phone, but no one answered."

"Did you try her cell?"

"Yeah, I was getting to that right now," Parker said while dialing his wife's cell number. There was no answer. Feeling very uncomfortable, Parker tried the home number again. This time his oldest son answered the phone. Without taking a moment to greet his son or make small talk, Parker asked, "Where's Mommy?"

"She left about thirty minutes ago," Parker Jr. said.

"Where did she go?"

"She went to the store to get more chocolate chips for the cookies."

"Oh, okay," Parker said somewhat relieved. "Have her call me when she gets back. How are you guys doing?"

"We're okay. Mommy made us grilled cheese. How's Auntie Teri? Did she have the baby yet?"

"Auntie is doing okay. She just went in to have the baby right now. I'll call you back after the baby is born. But have Mommy call me when she gets back."

"Okay, Daddy. I'll let her know."

No sooner than Parker had hung up his phone it rang back. The caller ID said 'home.' "Yes, son," Parker said answering the phone.

"It's me, honey," Noel said. "PJ said you called."

"Yes, I was calling to give you an update on Teri and the baby."

"Oh, how are they coming along? Did she have the baby already?" asked Noel excitedly. Parker could hear his son in the background telling his mother that his auntie did not have the baby yet.

"She is in the delivery room right now. I'll call back when she comes out. How are the cookies coming along?"

"Not so great. I burned the first batch. So, I had to go to the store to get more chocolate chips and eggs."

"Okay, let me let you guys get back to baking. I'll call you once the baby is here."

"Okay, Parker. I love you."

"I love you, too," Parker said before disconnecting the phone.

Trina was sitting there listening to Parker's entire conversation with his son and then with his wife. She could tell by his body language and the questions he asked his son that he really did not trust Noel. It was hard for her to see a man in pain. She could tell he really loves his wife. She hoped for his sake, he would not get his heart broken again by the chance he was giving his wife now.

When Parker turned around, he saw Trina watching him intently. He wondered what was going on in her mind. But, he decided not ask. He knew she had a slight crush on him. Instead, he asked, "How's Melvin?"

"He's doing great. Once the baby is here, he will make his way over."

"Yeah, I wonder how long that will be."

"As long as there are not any complications, it should not be long."

"Do you want to go down to the cafeteria and grab something to eat?"

"As a matter fact, I do. When Teri's water broke, we were right in the middle of having lunch. We did not even have an opportunity for them to wrap it up to go."

Parker and Trina made their way down to the cafeteria and found very slim pickings there. Trina opted for a fruit and yogurt parfait. Parker decided to be brave and try the roast beef sandwich.

"Do you know how long that sandwich has been sitting there?"

"No, but I figured since this is a hospital cafeteria, it shouldn't be too bad. They are interested in my health aren't they?"

"They may just be interested in getting more patients," Trina said laughing.

After biting into the sandwich Parker said, "You may have a point there." Pushing the sandwich away, he began to eye Trina's parfait.

"Don't even think about it, buddy," she said laughing.

"Oh, I see how it is," Parker said as he rose from his chair. He made his way back over to the refrigerated section and chose a parfait for himself. When he made it back to the table, Trina was still laughing.

"So, you decided to play safe this time did you?"

"Yes, I have three kids."

"And what? You want to hang around for them?"

"Yes, and I don't have any extra money for hospital bills," Parker said, having to laugh himself.

"You're such a good father."

"Well, I try. Teri and I didn't have that experience, and I don't want my children to suffer from not having a positive male role model."

"Yeah, I see how you are with them. I bet you are a good husband, too," Trina added.

"Sometimes I wonder."

"Wonder about what?"

"I wonder what made my wife's head turn towards another man."

"Sometimes, women don't know when they have it good. I'm sure other women wish they could be in her shoes."

"Anybody you know?" Parker asked, looking straight into Trina's eyes. They both knew he was asking about her. She had not made it any secret that she thought Parker was good looking.

"Let me put it to you this way. If I did not love my husband and I were not happily married, I would give Noel a run for her money."

"Is that so?"

"Yes, that's so. But because we are both married, I will leave it right there."

"Fair enough," Parker agreed. He was flattered by Trina's comments, but like her, he is faithful to his commitments.

After finishing their snacks, Parker and Trina headed back to the maternity ward. They hoped to receive some good news once they returned. When they stepped off the elevator, Priscilla was standing there wiping her eyes and blowing her nose.

"Mom, is everything alright?" Parker asked with concerned.

"Oh, yes. The baby is here. She is so beautiful, and she has a head full of dark curly hair. She is adorable. I wanted to hold her, but she is getting cleaned up and weighed."

"Oh, great," Parker said with relief. His mother's reaction alarmed him. But what didn't? He was really on edge these days.

"Is Teri back in her room yet?" Trina asked.

"If not, she will be soon."

"Did everything go okay with the delivery?" Parker asked.

"Oh, yeah. It was fine."

When the three of them arrived back to Teri's room, Reggie was waiting for them. He had just come from holding his new baby. The nurses were taking her footprints and filling out the birth certificate.

"Congratulations, man!" Parker said.

"Yes, congratulations, Reggie!" Trina chimed in. "Melvin is on his way."

"Yes, I just talked to him," Reggie said as he was totally focused on his phone.

"What has your attention on the phone?" Priscilla inquired.

"I am posting Regina's picture on my Facebook page."

"Oh, is that what you guys named her?" Trina asked.

"Yes, she was named after her daddy," he said sticking his chest out.

"What's her full name?" Parker asked.

"Regina Monae Langston."

"Awe, that's nice," Trina crooned.

"Yes, I like it, too. I had my hand in it as well. I chose Monae for her middle name," said the proud grandmother. "Reggie, are your parents coming to town soon?"

"I spoke with them earlier today. They will be flying in tomorrow."

"Oh, that will be nice. I haven't seen them in some time. I really miss spending time with your mom ever since they moved back east."

"I'm sure they will be happy to see you, too."

"I will make dinner for us one night while they are here. How long will they be in town?"

"They haven't made any definite plans, but I know Mom was talking about staying for a while to help Teri with the baby."

"That's great. I will get to see a lot of her then."

The nurse knocked on the door. "I have our new mommy here, everybody." The gang all clapped as Teri was wheeled back into the room. Right behind her came Baby Regina. They all asked Teri how she felt and cooed over the baby but were careful not to touch her. They did not want to spread their germs to her.

Melvin arrived to the hospital and went to the gift shop/flower shop and called his wife to meet him there. Together, they chose a beautiful arrangement of flowers and balloons and took them upstairs to the new parents. Everyone was celebrating new life and the love they had for one another. There was nothing but tears and smiles filling the room, plus a few baby noises here and there.

27

Reggie stayed overnight in the hospital with his wife and daughter, but the next morning he went to LAX to pick up his parents Reggie Sr. and Michelle. After taking his parents to his house and getting them settled comfortably into the guest room, Reggie returned to the hospital to pick up Teri and Regina. They were being discharged after one night's stay. When they returned home, to their surprise, Michelle had gone into the kitchen and prepared a nice dinner.

"Mom, I see you aren't wasting any time making yourself at home. Thank you so much. I was getting tired of eating hospital food."

"I had planned to cook some food and freeze it before the baby came," Teri said apologetically. "But she ended up coming a week early." She did not want her mother-in-law to think she wasn't taking care of her son, although Michelle had complimented her many times over the years of Teri's love and care for Reggie.

"Oh, it's no bother at all, sweetheart. I just want to be of help."

"Thank you. I appreciate it. If you need anything, let me know. I'm going to go upstairs and nurse the baby."

"Oh, Teri," Michelle began.

"Yes?"

"I called your mom. She'll be coming over for dinner."

"That sounds great. Honey, do you want to call Parker, Noel and the kids?"

"Will that be too much for you having all the kids here?" Reggie asked with concern.

"No, I'm actually feeling good. I am going to take a nap though right after I nurse the baby. Have them come over at about five tonight."

As Teri was napping, her mom arrived and continued helping Michelle in the kitchen to prepare dessert. As Teri slept, she began to have a quite disturbing dream. She dreamt someone went into the nursery and lifted her baby out of the crib. She tried fitfully to wake herself from the dream, but the dream persisted. When she was finally able to wake up, she found herself drenched with sweat. She began crying uncontrollably. She was crying so loudly Reggie heard her and raced up the stairs with Priscilla and Michelle right behind him.

"What is it, babe? What's wrong?"

"Bring me, Regina!" Teri screamed.

"Why, what's wrong?"

"I need to see her!" she said still crying and screaming.

"Baby, what's wrong?" Priscilla asked, rubbing her daughter's back.

Meanwhile, Michelle stepped into the master bathroom to grab a face towel from the linen closet. She moistened it with cold water, then walked over to Teri and Priscilla and began to wipe the sweat from her daughter-in-law's face. Reggie walked in with his sleeping daughter. When Teri saw her, she reached for her and held her tightly in her arms. The tears began to flow again.

"Let me have a moment alone with them, please," Reggie said to both mothers.

When they left the room, Reggie sat on the bed with his wife and daughter and embraced them both. "Are you aware that both of you mean everything to me? Please, tell me what is wrong."

"I had a nightmare that someone went into Regina's nursery and picked her up out of her crib."

"Well, honey you can see that she's okay. It was just a dream. You don't have to worry. I won't let anything happen to her or you for that matter."

"I know Reggie, but it really scared me. I just want to protect her from all the evil in the world."

"I know you do, but that is what fathers are for. With the two of us on her team, she can't go wrong. Why don't you lay back down and get some rest?"

"Okay, but leave her in here with me. Place her in the bassinet."

Reggie obeyed his wife's request and went back downstairs to explain everything to their parents.

"I should have known something like this could possibly happen," Priscilla said.

"How could you have possibly known something like that?" Michelle asked.

"I will explain it to you later," Priscilla said.

"It sounds like a bout of postpartum depression," Reggie Sr. said. Reggie Sr. had worked as a psychiatrist in his private practice before he retired three years ago.

"Well, let's not make diagnoses prematurely," Michelle said.

"Yes dear, but I don't think I'm wrong." Reggie, Priscilla, and Reggie's parents continued to discuss Teri's outburst for the next thirty minutes or so. Finally, they decided to let it rest.

About an hour later, Teri awakened and made her way downstairs. Parker and his family had arrived. She was happy to see her niece and nephews, and they were happy to see her also.

"Auntie, where's the baby?" Noella, her niece, asked.

"She's in the nursery in her crib," Teri answered. Reggie glanced over at her with a questioning look. "I put her there before I came downstairs," Teri continued.

"Can we see her, Auntie?" the children pleaded.

"Uncle Reg told us to wait until you were awake."

"Okay, then go ahead. Noel, can you take them?"

"Sure, plus I want to see her, too," Noel said.

After Noel and the children had gone upstairs, Teri pulled Parker into the kitchen to talk while she served herself some of the dinner Michelle made. The dishes in the sink told her everyone else had already eaten. "So, how are things at home, hon?"

"I really can't say, sis. I'm not good at gauging these things."

"Well, is she being more attentive to you? Do you notice any suspicious behavior?"

"She is definitely trying to be attentive. However I am really keeping my distance from her."

"Why's that?"

"I don't want to entangle myself emotionally more than I already am."

"Sounds like you're playing it safe just in case it doesn't work out the way you want it to."

"Yeah, I guess you could say that."

"Well, hon, you know relationships cannot be planned out exactly how we want them to be. There has to be an element of trust."

"Yeah, been there done that," Parker said sarcastically.

"Just give it some time," Teri advised.

"That's what Trina said."

"You talked to Trina about your marriage?"

"We talked briefly while we were at the hospital waiting for you to have the baby. Why? Was that a bad move?"

"No, just asking."

Reggie entered the kitchen and saw Teri and Parker talking. "I will join you guys, if that's okay."

"Yeah, sure," Parker answered. Reggie fixed himself a plate and sat at the island next to his wife.

"Having seconds?" Teri asked.

"Oh, no. I haven't eaten. I was waiting for you."

With a mouthful of food, Teri said, "Oh, I am so sorry. I saw all the plates in the sink, and I assumed everyone had eaten."

"No problem. What were you guys talking about?"

"The trials and tribulations of marriage," Parker said with a smirk on his face. "Do you have any advice, Reg?"

"Yeah, be true to yourself."

"What do you mean by that exactly?" Parker asked.

"Be yourself. Do what you feel is right. Don't let anyone change that. If you do anything contrary to what you believe, you may regret it later. If you want to be with Noel, be with her. And, don't do it halfway. Go all the way and see what happens. Don't let your fear hold you back."

"That's good advice, babe," Teri said as she listened to her husband with admiration. She knew it would be extremely hard for Reggie to bounce back if he were in Parker's shoes, but he didn't want his own biases to cloud Parker's judgment.

"I will take your advice. I think everything will work out," Parker said with a smile.

After Teri ate, it was time to nurse Regina again. Feeding the baby left her drained. Afterward, she went right back to sleep, she and the baby.

Meanwhile, her family packed up and left. This time when Teri slept, she slept soundly, no nightmares.

28

Reggie's parents stayed with them for one month. During that time, they were a great help to Teri as she became more and more accustomed to being a mother, nursing, and having her personal schedule altered.

Two weeks after her in-laws' departure, Teri had her six-week checkup. Dr. Iris gave her a clean bill of health.

"Teri, everything looks great. Will you be returning to work soon?"

"Yes, I plan to go back in two weeks. I will miss being with Monae every day, but I'm ready to get back into the swing of things."

"I thought your daughter was named after her dad," Sharon said with a confused look on her face.

"She is. I like to call her by her middle name though."

"Oh, okay. Also, I wanted to ask you about what we discussed during your last prenatal visit. Have you given anymore thought to talking with a therapist, either one-on-one or perhaps in a group session?"

"I have given it a great deal of thought, especially since having the last few episodes."

"What do you mean episodes?"

"Ever since I gave birth, I've been having nightmares about someone touching my daughter in her crib or taking her from it in the middle of the night."

"Are you sure that is related to your issues of abuse, or can it simply be postpartum depression?"

"I really don't know. My father-in-law thinks it is postpartum but knowing the dreams deal with my daughter's safety, I am thinking otherwise or maybe a combination of both. But, either way, I'm ready to move forward to dealing with my past and putting my insecurities behind me."

"I'm glad to hear that. You will be glad you did. I know I was. Like I told you before, therapy did wonders for my life."

"Can you give me the information for the sessions you hold?"

"I already have it ready for you," Sharon said as she reached into her pocket and pulled out a card with the session location, days and times.

"Thank you."

"Do you know when you will attend your first session?" Trying to be gentle as she pressed the issue a little more to spring Teri into action.

"It will probably be some time after I return to work."

"Great. I look forward to working with you in that capacity."

Two weeks later, Teri returned to work. Her mother would watch Regina during the day when Teri and Reggie were at work. Teri felt secure knowing her daughter was in safe hands, in a safe house, and in a safe environment free from predators and pedophiles.

On her first day back, Teri's time was more enjoyable than she could have imagined. She didn't have any patients to visit, so she spent her time making small talk with some of the nurses and other doctors and catching up on paperwork. Everyone wanted to see pictures of Regina. So, when they stopped by her office, Teri had them ready and available on her phone. She had what could be considered an entire photo album of her daughter's first two months of life. Also, her friend Denise, who loves to scrapbook, had made her a scrapbook of pictures. Teri just happened to have it with her just in case anyone wanted to take a look at it.

During her lunch hour, there was a small reception to welcome her back to the surgical unit and to the hospital. Those who were unable to attend the baby shower brought baby gifts, while others brought gifts especially for Teri. Someone even made a collage of Regina's pictures from Facebook and placed them in a frame for Teri to hang on a wall in her office. Everyone took turns telling stories about the different events that had taken place and the patients that had come into the hospital while Teri was on leave.

One story that was shared, Teri would not soon forget. "Teri, listen to this," one of the other doctors said. "You are not going to believe this one."

"Okay, get the story right, doc," one of the nurses blurted out, knowing his history of embellishing stories and getting the details twisted around. The crowd roared with laughter.

"I'm all ears, Steve," Teri said.

Steve continued, "During the graveyard shift, a cowboy came into the emergency room dressed in full gear."

"A cowboy?"

"Yes! And he had the strangest request."

"Wait, what do you mean full gear?"

"He had on a cowboy hat, jeans, gun holster, cowboy boots, and spurs."

"Was there a gun in the holster?"

"You better believe it! But, we aren't sure if it was real or not."

"Oh, no!" Teri screeched. "Well, what was his request?" she asked.

"Well, first of all, let me say he did not come in alone." After giving a slight pause for effect, Steve continued. "He brought his pit bull in with him."

"Huh? Why?" Teri asked, totally confused.

"Unfortunately, his dog had gotten shot, and he wanted the bullet removed."

"Did he not know that our hospital is for humans only?" one of the nurses asked.

"My question exactly," Teri commented.

"Apparently not, and apparently, he didn't care. He kept insisting that we save his dog. He even shed tears as he clutched his dog in both arms."

"When did he finally leave?"

"Not until the police got here and escorted him out."

"Oh, wow. That is really sad," Teri said.

"Yeah, but it gets worse," Dr. Karen Lozada said as she picked up the story to run with it.

"Oh, how much worse can it get than a cowboy and his shot dog?" Teri asked.

"How about the reason the dog got shot in the first place?"

"What was it a dog fight or something? You know pit bull owners are known for engaging their dogs in such activity."

"Well, it definitely was an activity, but I wouldn't exactly call it a fight," one nurse said.

"Not in so many words," another said laughing.

Teri's curiosity was getting the best of her. Her co-workers were having a blast teasing her and keeping her in suspense about the man and his dog. "Okay, you guys. What happened? You know I need to get back to my shift."

"What shift?" one doctor asked.

"You know all the patients she has," another chimed in.

"I didn't know one had patients while on maternity leave," a third said.

The teasing went around and around. All Teri could do was laugh with them. Finally, realizing they needed to get back to their own patients, they finished telling the story.

Karen picked up where she left off, "The reason the cowboy's dog was shot was because the cowboy took the dog down the street to where a female pit lives and allowed his dog to mount her. She was wailing so loudly, the owner came running outside. As the cowboy tried to get his dog unstuck from the girl, the owner ran back inside to get his gun. Just as the cowboy was trying to get out the gate, the owner fired at both of them. Luckily, the cowboy didn't get hit, but unfortunately, his dog did."

"Oh, my goodness," Teri said while laughing as she imagined the male dog mounted on the female and not wanting to turn her loose. "This was fun everyone. Thanks for welcoming me back." Each person took turns hugging Teri and letting her know she was truly missed.

Everyone finished lunch, Teri grabbed her gifts, and they all went back to their respective locations.

When Teri got home that night after picking of Regina at her mother's house, she was exhausted from being out for over eight hours. She hadn't been to the hospital in the capacity of an employee for six months. *Maybe I should have gone back part time first,* she thought. *Well, at least I don't have patients right now nor did I have a surgery scheduled, so I guess I shouldn't complain,* she thought.

Although she was exhausted, she still had plenty of energy to play with her baby girl. Oh, how she loved her daughter.

29

Once Teri re-acclimated herself to the work environment at Kaiser, after her six-month hiatus, she felt good being back into the swing of things. Five days a week she would go into work after dropping her daughter off at her mother's home. Afterward, she or her husband would pick Regina up. Sometimes though, Teri would be called in for emergency surgeries. Priscilla was always available to keep Regina in a moment's notice. Teri would either swing quickly by Priscilla's house, or Priscilla would go to her house if Reggie was not home to stay with Regina.

Once Teri was settled into her daily routine, she decided it was time to begin therapy. She desperately wanted the memories and the fears of the past to be extinguished. She wanted to be in full control of her emotions and had decided to not allow the past to have power over her any longer.

One Saturday morning, Teri reached into her purse and began to search for the business card Dr. Sharon Idris had given to her. Not being able to locate it, she quickly pulled out her cell phone and dialed Sharon's private line.

When Sharon saw her friend's number on her caller ID, she immediately knew what the call was about. "Hello, my friend," Sharon answered enthusiastically.

"Hey there. How are you doing this bright and beautiful Saturday morning?" Teri replied.

"I am doing well and just enjoying my day off from the hospital. In a couple of hours, I'll be getting ready for my evening therapy session with the ladies."

"Oh, great. That is exactly why I called."

"Are you ready to get started?" Sharon asked.

"Yes, I believe I am," Teri said without hesitation.

"Will you be able to make it tonight? Our session starts at 5 PM in Cathedral City."

"Yes, I can be there."

"Okay. I just have one question for you."

"Sure, what is it?"

"Have you spoken to your husband about the therapy sessions?"

"I spoke with him about it but not in detail."

"I suggest that you do."

"Is there any particular reason why?"

"Yes, because the sessions will probably unlock something with in you and potentially change your moods and temperament. It is always best that loved ones are prepared for this."

"Okay. I understand. I will speak with Reggie today before I go to the first session."

"Okay, so I will see you at five. Do you need the address?"

"Yes, I do. But before you give it to me, I have a question for you."

"Shoot."

"About how many women usually attend the sessions?"

"It varies. Sometimes the group is constant, while at other times, some women are transitioning out and new women like you come in. Tonight, I would say there will probably be about ten or twelve women in total. Do large crowds concern you?"

"In general, no. But I'm not sure how I will feel in this situation. But I am open to try."

"That is the right attitude. Have an open mind and see what happens."

"Okay. I will."

Before Sharon and Teri disconnected from their call, Sharon gave Teri the address for the session that would take place later that evening. When Teri hung up, she held the phone in her hands for a few moments. She couldn't believe she was moving forward with this. She was excited and nervous at the same time. After checking on Regina, who was sleeping soundly in her crib, Teri went to find Reggie. As she suspected, he was in the garage working on his Chevy. He had been working on that car for years and was finally bringing it to completion. When she opened the garage door, she found her husband standing with a rag in his hand a few feet away from his car with a grin that covered his face from ear to ear.

"Sorry to interrupt your love affair," Teri said with a little laugh. Reggie had no words to respond. He simply laughed along with her. Still admiring his car, it did not dawn on him that his wife actually wanted his attention.

"So, babe, you think we can talk for a minute?" Teri asked.

"Oh, sweetie, I'm sorry," Reggie said as he turned himself away from the bright red automobile.

"Do you remember I had mentioned possibly going to therapy sessions with Sharon?"

"Yes, I remember you bringing it up, but I didn't really think you were interested. Why?"

"I decided it would be best for me and all of us if I go."

"Okay."

"Is that all you have to say?"

"Yes. If you think it is best and it will help, I am in support of you. When are you going to begin?"

"Sharon is holding a session this evening at 5 PM. I thought I would go."

"Sounds good. Regina and I will be here watching the game."

Reggie, thinking the conversation was over, went back to polishing his car. However, Teri did not go back inside the house. When Reggie looked up again, she was still standing there. "Is there something else, babe?" Reggie asked.

"Yes, Dr. Idris said I should prepare you that after joining the sessions, my mood may change."

"What do you mean *change*?" Reggie asked with concern.

"I'm not exactly sure. I guess we will just have to wait and see."

"I'm not really sure I like the sound of that."

"I'm sure it's not as bad as it sounds."

"Well, do you think she means you may be more on edge because you're recalling memories?"

"Well, that's what I figured she meant."

"Okay, we will just deal with it as it happens- if it happens."

"Okay, sounds good."

Teri leaned over and kissed her husband and walked back inside to check on their daughter. Finding Regina sleeping soundly, Teri decided to go into the kitchen and make lunch. She pulled out bowtie pasta, pepperoni, salami, green and black olives, Italian salad dressing, green onions, pepper jack cheese, and tomatoes. She was preparing to make her famous pasta that her husband found delectable. She also took out the garlic bread spread, a mixture of mozzarella and mild cheddar cheeses, and two rolls of French bread to make her famous garlic bread. Then, reaching into the wine refrigerator, she selected a bottle of Stella Rosa red wine.

She had not been able to enjoy wine throughout the duration of her pregnancy and a couple of months afterward because of breastfeeding. Having difficulties with breastfeeding, she decided to hang it up. This would be her first day of enjoying a small glass of her favorite wine Stella Rosa.

By the time Reggie had made his way in from the garage, the kitchen was filled with aromas enticing enough to wet anyone's pallet. After moving quickly into the bathroom to wash his hands, Reggie seated himself at the island to partake of the lunch his wife had made. Teri watched her husband move quickly about the kitchen and take a seat. She could almost see his mouth salivating. She knew he loved her pasta and garlic bread. With a smile on her face, she served him a generous portion along with a tall glass of wine. Finally, she took a seat next to him with a plate of her own. They ate in virtual silence. The only things you could hear were forks clicking against the bottoms of the plates. When Reggie's plate was almost empty, Teri asked, "Would you like some more, honey?"

"You know I do," he answered." After Teri fixed her husband another serving, the silence continued.

After lunch was devoured and the kitchen cleaned, Reggie and Teri went to lie down for a nap while Regina was still sleep. With Regina being so young, she slept for two or three hours at a time. Her parents knew they had better take advantage of this opportunity to get a little rest themselves.

An hour later, Teri woke up to prepare for the evening session. She quietly opened her walk-in closet and selected a nice casual outfit. Having worn suits all week to work, she decided she just wanted to be comfortable. By the time she had finished dressing, her daughter awoke. Sitting in the nursery rocking chair, Teri fed Regina a warm bottle and sang softly to her. As she sang and looked down at her daughter, she realized how much of a difference therapy would make in both of their lives. Tears ran down her face.

Right at that moment, Reggie walked in. Seeing Teri's tears, Reggie immediately became concerned. "What's wrong, babe?"

"Nothing. Everything is right," Teri said with a smile. "I was just sitting here looking at our beautiful daughter and thinking about how much our lives will be better when I go through my healing and deliverance process. I'm ready for this." Reggie walked over and stood behind the rocking chair and gently massaged his wife's shoulders as he looked at his daughter's sweet face.

"There are only good things in store for us, Teri. I am glad that you are taking this step. I am here to support you 100%."

Thirty minutes later, Teri was pulling out of the garage with Reggie holding Regina and waving goodbye to her. Teri had a warm feeling inside, but anxiety was still present. She decided to calm her nerves by listening to praise and worship music as she drove down the freeway to Cathedral City. Locating the correct address, Teri pulled into the parking lot. Before going in, she decided to take several deep breaths. Finally after collecting herself, she got out of the car and walked over to the building.

Walking down the hallway, she surveyed the different rooms and the people inside. Finally, she approached the room where the meeting would be held, and just as she was about to open the door, Sharon walked out. They greeted each other with a hug. Sharon noticed Teri's slight apprehension and said, "Don't worry. You will be fine. Come on in."

Teri following her friend's command walked into the room and took a seat. The other women there began to welcome her and tell her their names. With a smile on her face, she reciprocated. She certainly felt welcome, and her nervous condition began to cease. As she smiled at the women, she kept repeating over and over in her mind, *God has not given me the spirit of fear but of power, love and a sound mind.*

Moments later, Sharon began the meeting with prayer and these words that she had the women to repeat, "I take authority over my life. I am not and will not be subjected to my past. The intrusions that occurred in my life and the abuse that was subjected upon me were not my doing and were not my fault. I am deciding at this moment that I will walk in true healing and deliverance. From this moment forward, I am set free."

After the women recited those statements, they all clapped and cheered and hugged one another. Then, they all took their seats and the meeting began. Sharon stated the purpose of the meeting and invited each woman to introduce herself to the group, even those who had been there numerous times before. After the introductions, Sharon shared her own personal testimony of abuse and then invited those who wanted to share their stories to do so. Teri sat quietly as woman after woman shared her testimony. Not all of them shared, but the majority of them did.

As the others listened as one person at a time spoke, tears were shed throughout the room as they witnessed the horrific details of what was being shared. After each woman shared, she was given an opportunity to express how she felt at the moment of the violation and even how she feels now years after the violation.

At the end of the night, Teri was completely horrified and sick to her stomach after she heard all the women's accounts from their past. Now, she had complete understanding of why Sharon had said her mood and temperament may be altered.

Leaving the session having not shared her own personal stories, Teri drove home in complete silence. She could not help but to replay what she had heard over and over and over again in her mind. She thought, *I don't know if this is going to help or make matters worse. But, I am going to trust Sharon's advice and stick with it.*

When she arrived home, she found Reggie lying across their bed with Regina cradled next to his stomach. When she saw that picture of love, all the feelings that she experienced from the time of the meeting and throughout her drive home dissipated.

30

The next week on Sunday, Teri, Reggie, and Regina went over to Priscilla's for a family dinner. Shortly after they arrived, Parker, Noel, and their three children made their entrance. Everyone loved the family dinners. This was their opportunity to get together and share everything that was going on in their lives. Anticipating her children's and her grandchildren's presence, Priscilla cooked an enormous dinner.

She pulled out all the stops. She made greens, cornbread, roast beef, ham, candied yams, corn-on-the-cob, mashed potatoes, a green salad, rolls, and plenty of sweet tea and punch for the kids. For dessert, she made a peach cobbler, pecan pie, and homemade ice cream.

As everyone gathered into the dining room, all the women helped to place the food on the table. Even four-year-old Noella, Parker's daughter, helped. The men and children sat there with their eyes as big as saucers. Everyone loved when Priscilla cooked.

After Reggie said grace, everyone dug in. As they ate, everyone was brought up to speed on what the others were doing. Reggie had begun a new project at *NASA*. And, of course, he was extremely excited. He loved being a *NASA* engineer. It was as if that was what he was always meant to do. Parker was transitioning from his job into a new one. Noel had recently been laid off from her job. They were doing cutbacks. But with her skills as an expert retail buyer, she should be able to get a new position in no time. She already had an interview lined up with Niemen Marcus for the next week. And, Teri filled her mother and brother in on her new adventure of therapy.

Using code language, she told them about her first session and how the women shared such devastating stories. Because the children were present, she didn't go into a lot of detail, but everyone understood the points she was making. Noella even decided to fill her aunt and uncle in on her latest adventure: She had started preschool. And, she was very excited about it. She told them she was a big girl now.

As they ate and continued to share, Noel's cell phone vibrated constantly. Parker was visibly irritated, but Noel acted as if nothing was occurring. She thought no one could hear the vibration coming from her purse.

"Why don't you just answer the damn phone?" Parker yelled out. Parker's outburst startled Noel. She just stared at him. "Why are you acting like you don't hear the phone ringing?"

"I hear it."

"Well then, answer it. Unless you don't want us to know who's calling you."

"It's probably just Mary."

"Well, answer it."

Noel bent down. And reached into her purse to retrieve her cell phone. When she bent down, her shirt lifted up, and there was a visible bruise on the lower part of her back. When Teri saw it, she gasped. That caught Parker's attention, and then he looked to see what his sister was staring at. Seeing the bruise, Parker immediately stood up.

"What happened to your back?" he yelled.

Noel stood straight up, turned around to face her husband with her hand on her back, and said nothing. She was obviously nervous. All of the agitation in the room caught the attention of the children. Parker Jr. spoke up first, "What's wrong, Mommy?"

"Yeah, Mom. What's wrong with your back?" his little brother asked. Noel burst into tears and ran from the room. Parker started to follow behind her, but Teri gently placed her hand on his arm and said, "Let me go. I will talk to her. You go outside and calm down."

"Sis, I've had enough."

"I understand, hon. But don't forget the kids are here. Go outside and get some air," she said in a low voice.

"I will go with him," Reggie chimed in.

The entire Sunday dinner was disrupted. Priscilla was left with the kids as her adult children disappeared in different directions. She decided to change the atmosphere and capture the children's attention.

"Who wants some of Granny's homemade ice cream," she asked them. One by one each of them said, "Me!"

Noel had walked outside to the backyard. Catching up to her, Teri put her arms around her and gave her a tight hug.

"Come on talk to me," Teri prodded. "What's going on?" Before Noel could answer, Teri moved behind her and lifted up her shirt and said, "Let me see." When she saw the severity of the large purple bruise that extended from the middle of her back to her lower back, Teri exclaimed, "Who did this?"

"Nobody. I bumped into the dresser."

"How did you bump into the dresser? Did someone push you?"

"No, I was trying to lift something, and I fell backwards."

"If that is true, how come Parker did not already know about it?"

"I didn't want him to bother with it. I'll be fine."

"Noel, you don't have to lie to me. Have you been seeing that guy again? Did he do this to you?"

With Teri's questions, all Noel could do was begin to cry again. To Teri, that was a sign that she was on to something with her current line of questioning. She then pulled Noel over to the bench that was placed against the back wall of the house. They sat down, Teri placed her hand under Noel's chin, lifted it up, looked into her eyes, and said, "Tell me what's going on. I want to help you. But I can't help you if I don't know anything or if you lie to me."

"Okay, you're right. He did do this to me."

"So, you have been seeing him again or was it that you never stopped?" Teri asked with an attitude. She wasn't sure she was going to like what her line of questioning would turn up.

"Yes, I did stop, but he continued to call me and threaten me."

"What do you mean threaten you?"

"He said if I did not continue to see him, he would hurt my children."

"Oh, my goodness. Does he know where you live?"

"No, he doesn't, and that's why I quit my job."

"I thought you were laid off."

"No, I quit because he kept harassing me at work. And I know he can get to my personnel records and get my address."

"Personnel records are confidential."

"Yes, but he is sleeping with the human resources clerk."

"So, he started seeing her after you guys broke up?"

"I really don't know. He may have been seeing both of us at the same time."

"Okay, well that's another story. Have you told your husband about this?"

"No."

"Why not?"

"You know your brother's temper. He would hurt someone."

"So, you think it's better to be threatened and to get hurt yourself rather than let your husband help you?"

"I don't think it's fair to him to clean up a mess I made."

"Yeah well, that's the only thing you said so far that makes sense. So are you sleeping with this guy?"

"No, I'm not."

"So when exactly did you get that bruise?"

"I got it last week on my last day at work. It happened in the break room when he cornered me and tried to kiss me."

"Were there any witnesses?"

"Not that I know of. We were alone in the room."

"I think you need to tell your husband what's going on."

"At this point, I am inclined to agree with you. Can you ask him to come back here?"

"Sure." Teri walked back through her mother's house to the front yard where her brother and her husband were. As she approached them, she could hear her brother still raving mad. He was telling Reggie, "Man, I cannot deal with this. I am ready for a divorce now. She doesn't know whom she's playing with. She thinks he did some damage to her. Wait until I get my hands on her."

Reggie responded, "Man, don't do that. It's not worth it. Remember you have kids to think about." Teri jumped in right at that moment.

"Hon, Noel is in the backyard. She wants to see you. I really think you should listen to what she has to say. I don't think it's what you suspect. But you need to calm down first."

Parker was walking in circles and waving his arms. There seemed to be no calming him down. Teri went back inside the house and got their mother.

"Mom, please go out there and talk to your son. I can't reach him right now. I will stay with the kids. Plus, I need to feed the baby."

Priscilla walked outside, and five minutes later, she, Reggie, and Parker walked back in. Reggie and Priscilla stayed inside while Parker made his way to the backyard where his wife was waiting for him. From what Teri could gather, her brother was a lot calmer than he had been just minutes before.

When Parker reached the backyard, he walked over to Noel and sat next to her on the bench. He really did not want to look at her. He did not know what was going on, and he was really hesitant to find out. He did not know if his heart could take any more pain from her. But with all the courage that he could muster up, he looked her in the face.

"Please, tell me what's going on. How did you get that bruise on your back?"

"Paul did it."

"When Noel?"

"On my last day at work."

"Did it happen at work or somewhere else?" He braced himself for her answer.

"It was at work in the break room."

"Okay. So what happened?"

"Well, the long and short of it is he had been harassing me to get back together with him. He said he would hurt the kids if I didn't comply." With those words, Parker immediately jumped to his feet and faced his wife.

"What do you mean hurt the kids?"

"I'm not exactly sure what he meant by that, but I did not want to find out. That's why I quit my job, so I could get away from him."

"Oh, you quit your job?"

"Yes, I quit my job, and I'm sorry that I lied about that. I thought I was doing what was best, so you would not have to be involved, and we could just move on and get our lives back on track. Parker, I love you, and I want us to work out. I'm sorry I brought all of this on us."

"Let me see your back." Noel turned around lifted up her shirt and showed her husband the bruise. When he saw it, he immediately felt her pain. He wanted to hurt Paul for putting his hands on his wife. When he tried to touch the bruise, Noel jumped and winced in pain.

At her response, he turned her towards him and gently caressed her. She wept softly in his arms feeling undeserving of his comfort.

"Come on. Let's get the kids and go home." Noel simply nodded, took her husband's hand, and allowed him to lead her back into the house. She went into the restroom to clean her face, as not to worry the children.

"Is everything okay?" Priscilla asked.

"Yes, everything is fine," Parker responded.

"Are you sure?" Teri inquired.

"Yes, and thank you for talking to her. I really appreciate it."

"Anytime, hon. That's what sisters are for." Teri and Parker gave each other a hug. And when Noel came out the bathroom, Teri gave her a hug also.

"Thanks, sis," Noel said.

"Anytime," Teri responded.

After bundling up their children and saying goodbye to everyone, Parker and his family headed home. Not much later, Reggie and Teri bundled up Regina, said their goodbyes to Priscilla, and made their way home as well.

When Teri and Reggie had made it home and had tucked their daughter in bed, Teri just wanted to feel the warmth of her husband's arms. She could not imagine what her brother and his wife were going through or feeling. She just knew she never wanted to feel that type of separation from Reggie, and she told him so as she laid her head softly on his chest and felt the warmth from his body. Reggie knew what she was thinking. He held her gently and close to let her know he would always be there for her, and she needed not worry herself about that.

31

On Monday, after Teri had made her rounds at the hospital, she stopped into Sharon's office to have a quick chat. She wanted to share her impressions and concerns about Saturday's meeting. When she arrived at Sharon's office, Sharon was busy with a patient. When she finished, she walked out of the office and noticed Teri sitting quietly in the waiting room.

"Dr. Langston, it is so good to see you," she said. Teri was so deeply focused in her own world that she barely saw her friend approach her. Finally feeling someone's presence, Teri looked up, stood to her feet, and embraced her colleague. "You looked to be a million miles away," Sharon said.

"Yes, I was deep in thought."

"A good thought I hope."

"Actually, my thoughts were mixed."

"Do you care to share?" Sharon inquired.

"Yes, actually. I wanted to speak to you about the session the other night. If you have a moment."

"Sure, come on into my office," Sharon invited. Once the two women were settled in Sharon's office, Teri began to share her experience with her first therapy session.

"First, let me thank you for making me aware of the therapy sessions you hold. I believe they will be very beneficial to my overall state of being."

"Does that mean you enjoyed the session?" Sharon queried.

"Yes, I enjoyed the session very much."

"That is good to hear," Sharon encouraged. "However, I noticed you opted not to share."

"That is precisely what I want to speak with you about. I don't know that I am ready to speak about my past in an open forum. I have never heard myself articulate any of the incidents aloud with anyone other than my husband. Before I share with the other women and receive their comments or expressions, I think I would rather first articulate everything that transpired in a one-on-one session before the group session."

"That is perfectly understandable," Sharon agreed.

"Good. So is there some way I can do that?"

"Absolutely. I can set up a one-on-one session for you."

"That sounds great, but whom would the session be with?"

"Well, Teri, I do one-on-one sessions, but if you prefer, I can set you up with one of my colleagues."

"Oh, no. I definitely prefer to have a session with you. I trust you and your expertise."

"Very well then. What day is good for you?"

"I am eager to continue what I started, so when is your first available appointment?"

"Well, I have an opening for this afternoon at 4 PM. Will that work for you?"

"Can you give me a moment to check with my mom and my husband to make sure my daughter is taken care of?"

"Absolutely. I will give you some privacy while you make your call. As a matter of fact, there is another patient waiting for me. So, I will check in on her, and I'll come right back."

"Sounds good, Sharon. Thank you."

"No worries. It is my pleasure."

When Sharon returned to her office, Teri had already completed her calls. "So will four o'clock work for you, Teri?"

"Yes, the baby is all set, and I can stay around. Where can we meet?"

"Well, everyone will be gone from the office, so we can meet here if you like."

"Sounds good to me. I will see you later then," Teri said as she rose from her seat.

Sharon walked Teri to the office door, and they said their goodbyes. Sharon was proud of her friend for making this step in her life. She knew the difference that it had made because she had been there herself. She just prayed that the outcome would be the same for Teri as it had been for her.

After Teri left Sharon's office, she felt exhilarated about this new chapter in her life. Even though she had always held a positive outlook on life, she had more reasons now to be hopeful about her future and that of her family.

On her next break, she called her husband and discussed her therapy plan in detail. Her excitement made him excited for her. Unbeknownst to Teri, Reggie had planned a special dinner for her, but he didn't even bother to tell her because he felt the therapy session was far more important. *I will just schedule it for another night*, he thought to himself.

After leaving Sharon's office, Teri had lunch and visited all of her patients once again and closed her office down for the day. Before going upstairs to Sharon's office, she called her mother to check in on her baby girl.

"She was a little fussy today," Priscilla said.

"What do you mean, Mom?" Teri asked.

"For a while, she did not want to take her bottle, and she was running a slight fever."

"Did you give her some of the baby Tylenol or her Pedialite?"

"Yes, of course," Priscilla snapped. She did not particularly care for her children questioning her grand-parenting abilities.

"Well, is she doing any better after that?" Teri asked, ignoring her mother's irritability.

"Yes, I was finally able to get her to sleep."

"What is she doing now?"

"Right now, I have her in her swing. The other kids have gone home for the day. So, it is just she and I."

"Well, Reggie will be there in about an hour to relieve you."

"Oh, that's fine. You know I don't mind keeping her at all. I like the company," said Priscilla a lot calmer.

"I know, Mom. And, I really appreciate you more than you know. Mom, I have to run. I have my appointment with Sharon in about ten minutes. I need to get upstairs."

"Okay, dear. Let me know how everything went."

"I will. I will call you on my way home."

Ten minutes later, Teri was standing at Sharon's office door. Just like Saturday evening, she had butterflies in her stomach. *I can do this. I can do this,* she said to herself. As if she didn't know what was on the other side of the door, she pushed the door open very slowly. When she walked in, the first thing she noticed was Sharon was not wearing her white lab coat. Also, she had lit several candles and placed them around her office. The atmosphere was so serene. It was very different from just a few hours earlier when Teri had stopped by. She could tell Sharon had created the ambience to make her comfortable. Teri appreciated the gesture, and it was actually working. Her ball of nerves unraveled almost instantaneously.

"Come on in and make yourself comfortable," Sharon invited.

"Thank you. Where should I sit?" Teri asked as she looked around from the chairs to the sofa.

"Wherever you will feel most comfortable," Sharon suggested. Making a quick decision, Teri chose to sit in one of the armchairs. Easing her way into the conversation, Sharon decided to make small talk. "So, how was the rest of your shift?"

"It went rather smoothly. How was yours?"

"It went without a hitch. And that is something I cannot always say in my line of business." They both had to stop and laugh on that note. Teri knew exactly what her colleague meant. They had to always be prepared for the unexpected.

"I know what you mean," Teri said. "But look, Sharon, we don't need to belabor the point. I know your time is precious as well as mine, and I am truly ready to get started."

"Very well," Sharon agreed. "Let's begin. Where would you like to start?"

"Well, you are the expert, so I will take your lead."

"Let's begin with prayer," Sharon suggested. Teri didn't respond verbally; she simply bowed her head. At that moment, Sharon began to pray a fervent prayer.

After the prayer, Sharon asked again, "Where do you want to begin?"

"I think I want to start with the question you asked me when I came into the emergency room at the beginning of the trial."

"You mean the question that I asked about whether or not you had been pregnant before?"

"Yes, I want to start there. I did not tell you the entire truth."

"Okay, go ahead."

"The truth of the matter is I was raped by my friend's boyfriend when I was thirteen years old."

"Did you tell anyone at the time that it occurred?"

"No, I did not. I did not want to get in trouble with my mother for being over his house. I thought it better to allow her to think that I was sleeping around, which is what she accused me of."

"Why were you at his house?"

"My friend, his girlfriend, was there. I went over there to see her, and he said he wanted to show me something inside."

"Okay. Getting back to your mother. Weren't you concerned about the image that your mother would have of you by thinking you were sleeping around?"

"Actually, I was too young to know anything about other people's perception of me or even about forming a self-image of myself. Now in retrospect, I absolutely would have told her the truth and not allowed my character to be painted in that light."

"Whose decision was it for you to have the abortion?"

"It was my mother's decision, and I went along with it."

"Do you regret the decision?"

"Well, I cannot say that I would have wanted to have a child at that age, but at the same time, I believe the decision should have been mine. It was not anyone's decision to make about what I should do with my body or with my baby."

"Do you harbor any ill feelings toward your mother for the decision that she made for you?"

"At the time, I think I did, but I did not become aware of my feelings toward her until years later. Today though, I do not harbor ill feelings. I have forgiven her."

"Have you and your mom ever had a conversation about the abortion?"

"No, we have not."

"Do you ever think you will?"

"I don't know; maybe one day. Do you think it is essential to my healing process?"

"Yes it is because you need to forgive. Forgiveness unburdens us from a lot of dead weight and bondage. When we forgive others of their trespasses, we feel a lot freer. And we are able to love them and trust them in spite of their faults. Do you believe your mother had your best interest at heart?"

"Yes, I do. And because of that reason, I was able to forgive her. I know she had children at a young age, and she was only trying to protect me from going along the same path and living a life of hardships."

"Since we are talking about forgiveness, is there anyone whom you have not forgiven?"

"No one that I can think of. I have actually given that a lot of thought from time to time, and I have not come up with anyone that I have not forgiven."

"That's good. So, you've gone through the forgiveness process as it relates to your past issues of abuse."

"Yes, I have. My pastor preached a sermon some years ago about forgiveness, and it was at that point that I decided to forgive all of my abusers."

"From your last statement, it sounds like there have been more than one incident of abuse in your life."

"Yes, that is true."

"Would you like to share any other incidents at this time?"

This type of question and answer and reflection continued on for the next hour and a half. At the end of the session, Teri felt exhilarated and at the same time emotionally drained. The only thing she wanted to do was find a quiet place to lie down and cry. In the past, she had experienced these same emotions; however, she had not allowed herself to cry. She had always felt crying made the incidents real; whereas, not crying demonstrated her strength. She had not realized crying was actually a method of cleansing her soul.

Knowing what she was feeling, Sharon offered her a moment to lie on the couch. Teri eagerly accepted the invitation. Sharon handed her a box of Kleenex and walked out of the office, giving her a moment of privacy. Teri cried deep, deep sobs, and in doing so, she released her innermost pressures and feelings of helplessness. When she was done, she cleaned her face, thanked Sharon for the session, got in her car, and drove home to her husband and daughter.

When she arrived home, she greeted them with hugs and kisses. And, they lovingly returned them. Overall, it was a good day.

32

Later that week, after Priscilla dropped Parker's older two children off at school, she, Regina, and Parker's youngest son, Gary, were making their way back to her home. While they were stopped at a red light, Regina began to scream at the top of her lungs. Priscilla reached her arm back over the front seat to rub Regina's belly, in an attempt to soothe her. Just as Priscilla's hand reached Regina, Priscilla felt something pop near her elbow. She let out a scream herself. The pain was excruciating. Holding her elbow, she looked in her rear view mirror at the two children who were depending on her for care. Regina continued to wail, and Gary had his attention focused on his granny.

"What's wrong, Granny?" he asked. "Why did you scream, and what's wrong with Gina? Why is she crying? Do you think she wants her bottle, Granny? Huh? Do you?"

"Gary, I hurt my arm. Can you look in Gina's diaper bag and get her a bottle?"

"Yes, Granny."

While, Priscilla continued to drive home while holding her arm, Gary retrieved one of Regina's bottles and gave it to her. He liked being the big cousin and helping his granny take care of the baby. Finally, he wasn't the baby any longer.

When Priscilla pulled into her driveway, which was just a few blocks from the children's school, she didn't bother to try and get out of the car. She knew she couldn't carry Regina's car seat inside.

"Gary, take your seatbelt off, open your door, and come up here to the front seat."

"Take my seatbelt off?" Gary asked, as children do to verify their instructions.

"Yes, honey. Take your seatbelt off. Hurry. I need you." After trying for half a second, Gary said, "I can't get it off." Priscilla's arm was in so much pain, tears began to run down her face. She knew she had to have patience with her young grandson. He was only two and a half years old.

"Please try, Gary. Granny needs your help." The change in Priscilla's voice told Gary something was wrong. But, before he could respond, Mr. Coleman from next door walked over. He had been watering his grass when Priscilla drove up. He had waved to her but received no response. Then, he noticed she was just sitting in the car, making no attempt to get out.

"Is everything okay, Priscilla," he queried.

"Hello, Dylan. I'm afraid it's not. I felt something pop in my arm. And, it hurts like the dickens."

"Do you think it's broken?"

"I don't know. It may be sprained."

"Okay, let me help you into the house."

"Oh, no. I can't move. My arm hurts too much. I need my phone. Can you go to the other side of the car and get my phone from my purse?"

"Sure," Mr. Coleman said as he quickly made his way around to the other side of the car. By that time, Gary had finally taken his seatbelt off.

"I got it off now, Granny."

"That's okay, honey. Mr. Coleman will do it."

"But I wanted to do it," he said whining, sounding like he was about to cry.

"Gary, Granny needs you to be a big boy. Stay there, and help Granny with your cousin. Is she finished with her bottle?" Priscilla asked to divert Gary's attention. Gary got on his knees to check on his baby cousin.

"Not yet, Granny," he reported.

Meanwhile, Mr. Coleman had retrieved Priscilla's phone. "Whom do you want to call," he asked, holding the phone ready to dial.

"Call Reggie." Once Mr. Coleman had Reggie on the phone, he promptly handed the phone to Priscilla. "Reggie, it's Priscilla."

Hearing the agony in her voice, Reggie asked, "Mom, what's wrong? Is it Regina? Is the baby okay?"

"Reggie, the baby is fine. It's me. I may have sprained or broken my arm."

"Okay, where are you now?"

"I'm at home in my driveway. I just dropped off the kids at school."

"Okay, where are Regina and Gary?"

"They are with me; they are in the backseat. Reggie is it possible that you can leave work? I really think I need to go to the hospital."

"I'm leaving now. I'm on my way. Have you called Teri?"

"No, not yet. I wanted to make sure you were able to get here. I know she has one or two surgeries scheduled for today."

"Okay, I will call her on my way there. Oh, who was that that I was talking to before you got on the phone?"

"That was my next-door neighbor Mr. Coleman."

"Oh, okay. Is he able to stay with you and the kids until I get there?"

"Dylan, can you stay with me until my son-in-law gets here? It will take him about twenty-five minutes."

"Sure, no problem," Mr. Coleman answered.

"Yes, he can," Priscilla said into the phone.

"Okay, I will see you soon," Reggie said.

As Reggie made his way over to Priscilla's, he tried to reach Teri, but it was to no avail. While Priscilla waited for Reggie to arrive, Mr. Coleman went inside his house and made an ice pack for Priscilla's arm. By the time Reggie arrived, the ice had not yet been able to cause the pain to subside. If anything, the pain grew increasingly worse and a bruise had formed around Priscilla's elbow. From what Reggie could tell, Priscilla needed to go to the emergency room right away.

He quickly grabbed Gary and Regina, in her car seat, and put them in his car. Mr. Coleman helped Priscilla get into the front seat of Reggie's car. Before they knew it, they were at the hospital. They pulled up to the emergency room door and an attendant helped Priscilla into a wheelchair and took her right in.

Meanwhile, Teri had returned Reggie's call and met them at the emergency room. Fortunately, she had finished her last surgery of the day and was able to take the rest the day off to see after her mother. While Reggie and the children sat in the waiting room, Teri went in to see the doctor with her mom. Because of Teri's presence, Priscilla received extra special attention.

After taking an x-ray of Priscilla's arm, it was found that she had a fracture of the ulna. By the time Priscilla left the emergency room, her arm had been secured in a cast.

Both Teri and Reggie went to Priscilla's house after leaving the hospital. Baby Regina rode with her mother and grandmother, while Gary rode with his uncle. They all made it back in time to pick up the other two children from school.

Once the children had been settled, fed their afterschool snack, and asked all their questions about Granny's cast, Priscilla, Reggie, and Teri discussed the possible reasons for why Priscilla's arm had been fractured from just reaching behind her seat. It was very curious to all of them, and they wanted some answers. In the emergency room, no answers could be provided. The only thing the emergency room doctor could suggest was for Priscilla to make an appointment with her general practitioner to have some tests run.

Later that afternoon, after Reggie and Teri had left and after Parker had come by to pick up his children, Priscilla called her doctor to make an appointment. Surprisingly, he had an opening for the next day.

During her doctor visit the next day and explaining how she sustained the ulna fracture, Priscilla was given the gold standard for osteoporosis diagnosis- a combination of [assessing] clinical risk factors and a bone mineral density assessment by dual-energy X-ray absorptiometry. Her doctor Vandalerro Ochoa said, "Your x-rays show signs of bone loss. This condition is called osteoporosis. Were you aware that you are calcium deficient?"

Priscilla was very surprised to hear the news. "No, I was not aware, and I find it very surprising because I take calcium supplement and drink milk regularly with my grandchildren. Also, I just had my physical less than a year ago, and I was given a clean bill of health."

"Unfortunately, Ms. Darling, bone conditions, such as osteoporosis, are not identified or detected during the annual physical. In most cases, they are not detected until situations like yours occur."

"Now that we have detected the problem, what can be done to fix it? Can osteoporosis be treated? Is it something that I can overcome or will I always have it?"

Dr. Ochoa said, "Your bones form the framework for your body. They allow you to sit, to stand, and to walk. They protect the vital organs inside your body, like your heart and lungs. Postmenopausal osteoporosis is a condition that weakens bones over time, making them thinner, more brittle, and more likely to break. Every woman past menopause should make strengthening her bones a priority. Postmenopausal osteoporosis is a common form of osteoporosis. In fact: Up to 20% of bone loss happens in the five to seven years just after menopause. One in two women over age fifty will have an osteoporosis-related fracture in her lifetime. Once you've had a fracture, your chances of having another are much higher. A fracture can be a life-changing event. It can make it harder to get around and do things on your own. That's why it's so important to take steps now to manage your postmenopausal osteoporosis."

"How do I manage it?"

"I am going to prescribe Prolia for you."

"What type of drug is that?" Priscilla asked with great concern.

"It is a prescription medicine used to treat osteoporosis in women after menopause who are at high risk for fractures."

"Are there any side effects that I should know about?"

"Well, there are several although they are uncommon. The side effects and risks include low blood calcium. Take calcium and vitamin D to help prevent low blood calcium. Serious allergic reactions, including low blood pressure (hypotension); trouble breathing; throat tightness; swelling of your face, lips, or tongue; rash; itching; or hives. Serious infections in your skin, lower stomach area (abdomen), bladder, or ear may happen. Inflammation of the inner lining of the heart (endocarditis) due to an infection may also happen more often in people who take Prolia. Prolia is a medicine that may affect your immune system. People who have weakened immune systems or take medicines that affect the immune system may have an increased risk for developing serious infections. Skin problems such as inflammation of your skin (dermatitis), rash, and eczema have been reported. Severe jaw bone problems (osteonecrosis) may occur, as well as unusual thigh bone fractures."

"Wow! That is a lot to take in."

"Yes, it is. But, I will give you some literature to read to re-iterate everything I have said."

"Okay, I will have my daughter go over it with me."

"Very well. Here is your prescription."

Priscilla stopped by the pharmacy and then made her way home. She promptly called her son and her daughter and asked them to bring their families over to her house that evening. They both consented, and at six o'clock, everyone showed up to Priscilla's house. Not really being able to cook or wanting to maneuver with her new cast, Priscilla popped a pan of Stouffers lasagna in the oven. When Teri arrived, Priscilla asked her to make a tossed green salad to go with the lasagna. Teri readily consented and immediately got to work on the salad. She could tell from her mother's disposition that the reason she asked them over was not so pleasant. However, Teri decided not to impose. She would allow her mother share the news in her own time and in her own way.

After Teri finished preparing the salad and took out some dinner rolls, everyone sat around the table to enjoy the meal. Everyone made light conversation, but was eager to hear why Priscilla had called them over. About halfway through the meal, Priscilla finally decided to share.

"Okay, everybody. I know you have been waiting for me to share my news with you." No one answered verbally. Each person only nodded his/her head. So, Priscilla continued.

"I was diagnosed with osteoporosis today."

"I'm sorry, Mom," Teri responded.

"Is that what caused your arm to break?" Parker inquired.

"Yes, I was told my bone density is about 5% lower than what it should be," Priscilla responded.

"Is there anything that can be done about it?" Reggie wanted to know.

"They prescribed Prolia. It should help increase my bone density over time."

"I've heard about Prolia. I will do some research and find out the benefits and side effects," Teri offered.

All of Priscilla's children let her know they loved her and cared for her deeply, and they would be there to take care of her every step of the way.

33

Reggie and his colleagues were really enjoying the new project. The information was top-secret, so it had not yet been released to the public. Every day, and sometimes late into the evening, Reggie and his colleagues would discuss the plans on the project. There was talk that if the engineers could pull off the project successfully, there may be a promotion in it for some of them. That bit of information excited Reggie even more, and he figured while his wife was doing something to improve her quality of life by going to therapy, he would do the same by fully engaging in this project and securing more valuable information that would assist in his job performance.

After working with *NASA* for over nineteen years, he felt another promotion was well over due. He was therefore determined to do everything in his power to be one of the ones to gain a promotion. If it meant working late, so be it. If it meant working on the weekend, so be it. He did not want to work the same way he had been in the next ten years. He loved what he did, but he believed he had put in enough time that he should begin to solidify his retirement. After another ten or eleven years, he would be ready to hang up his hat.

With this new frame of mind, Reggie found himself working many, many long hours. This did not go unnoticed by his wife. There would be days when she would have an evening surgery, and the baby have to stay with her mother because both she and her husband were working. She thought it was awesome that Regina was able to spend so much time with her maternal grandmother; however, she had always thought that during these precious months in her daughter's life, either she or her husband would be with her. As the days and weeks went by, Teri became more and more concerned that her husband was not at home like he used to be.

One weekend, while they were fortunate enough to have dinner together, Teri thought it would be a good idea to bring it to Reggie's attention. After lighting the candles and putting the crystal plates on the table and pouring a chilled glass of wine, Teri turned her full attention to her husband. However, she did not immediately begin to speak. She wanted to wait for the right moment, and she did not feel it had arrived. After a few minutes had passed, she noted Reggie's attention was tuned into his cell phone, so she decided she needed to speak up. Otherwise, the cell phone would have won the competition for her husband's attention.

Breaking the silence, Teri asked sarcastically, "Do you think it's possible you could tear yourself away from the cell phone for at least a moment?"

Noting his wife's irritation, Reggie immediately turned the phone off and placed it in his pocket. "Sorry, dear. I know I have been preoccupied with work."

Interrupting him, Teri said, "Yes, you have. When are things going to return back to normal?"

"I don't know. I really can't say at this moment. We are still only midway through this project," Reggie said calmly.

"So, what you're telling me is the long hours and the neglect is going to continue."

"Long hours, yes. But what is this neglect you're talking about? Do you feel I have been neglecting you?" Reggie asked with all patience aside.

"Do you feel that you haven't?"

"Teri, don't answer a question with a question. Just answer me plainly."

"Okay, Reggie. Yes, you have been neglecting me. And it's not just me, but you have been neglecting our daughter as well."

"I don't think that's fair."

Interrupting him again, "You don't think what's fair?"

"You bringing our daughter into this."

"Reggie, I'm not bringing her into this. She is already in it. She has been spending more time at my mom's than we had planned.

"So, it's okay for you to work late, but not for me?" Reggie interjected.

"Reggie, don't be silly. You have a set 9 to 5 schedule. And I have a set schedule, unless I am on call. We both know that. You on the other hand..." Teri paused, not liking where the conversation was going.

Reggie took the opportunity to jump in. "Look Teri, you are right. I have been working long hours, and I apologize for any neglect I have portrayed towards you and the baby. It is neither my intent nor my objective to neglect either of you. I am only trying to secure a promotion and solidify my retirement. I am forty-one years old, and I do not plan to continue to work the way I have been for the rest of my life. In another ten years, I will be over fifty. I want to be able to attend all of Regina's events and enjoy the rest of my years with you."

Reggie's words softened Teri's heart. She had planned to really let him know how she felt. She did not like the feeling she had been having over the last couple of weeks, and she did not want it to persist. It had bothered her so much that she had even spoken to her mother about it. And, of course, her mother told her to go home and talk to her husband about it. She had put it off for a couple of days, but the opportunity had finally presented itself.

After Reggie's comment, Teri's heart melted and everything she had been thinking went totally out the window. She knew her husband loved her, and she certainly loved him. At the same time, she also knew how easily couples can drift apart, especially when they are not paying attention to their relationship. She did not care to be one of the statistics.

After releasing all the feelings she had bottled up, she turned her attention to the wonderful dinner she had picked up from Panda Inn. For the rest of the night, Reggie and Teri enjoyed the wonderful dinner and pleasant conversation. Rather than bickering and finding fault with one another, they enjoyed each other's company and shared the latest updates in their lives they had been too busy to share because of the long hours they had been working. Even though they enjoyed their professions, both of them were equally excited to have a day off.

"You brought up a good point about us not spending a lot of time together lately," Reggie said. "Did you realize that we did not take our annual vacation last year?"

"Yes, I did realize that, but we could not have taken it because I was pregnant."

"Yes, and that is my point exactly. It is almost summertime again, and we have not even mentioned what we're going to do this year."

"Well, I didn't know if we were actually going to take vacation this year with Regina being so young."

"If we begin to make excuses now, we will continue to make excuses each year as she grows older. We will always find a reason not to go rather than a reason to go. I believe we should keep our same tradition, and when she gets older, she can begin to join us- once in a while."

"You know- I like the way you think. So where do you want to go?"

"As usual, I will leave that up to you. Planning is your niche, and I'm going to leave it to you."

"Okay, well I'm on it. But I do have a question for you."

"What is that?"

"Will you be done with your special project by July?"

"We should be. It shouldn't take us more than another month or a month and a half."

"Okay, I will call the travel agent and begin planning. You just make sure you show up and get on the plane or the ship."

With that, they started laughing, picked up their glasses and clicked a toast.

34

A couple of weeks later, after things slowed down at work, Teri was ready to go back to the group therapy session. She felt really good about her one-on-one session with Sharon Idris, and after her emotional release, she was ready to share in the group.

When the group met on a Saturday evening, Teri was one of the first women to show up. After the opening prayer, the declaration, and the personal introductions, Teri volunteered to share her personal testimony. She actually surprised herself. Before going to the session, she knew she would share; however, she had no idea that she would volunteer to go first. But when she did, she held up her end of the bargain.

She shared the episodes of sexual abuse that began when she was only three years old and how they continued up to the time when she was thirteen years old. Unlike some of the other women, all of her instances of abuse were from different people and were not continuous, with one exception. They occurred sporadically throughout that ten-year time period. However, that did not make the incidents any less traumatic. If anything, she may have been even more traumatized because the incidents occurred when she was least expecting them. Whereas, someone who was abused on a regular basis pretty much knew when the abuse was going to occur and by whom.

After Teri finished sharing, some of the women had questions for her. At first, she was a little uneasy answering the questions, but as the evening wore on, she became more and more comfortable with sharing. As she answered the women's questions, they also opened up and shared their experiences as well. What Teri really liked about the session was that not one person was put on the spot, but each person engaged equally.

When the session ended, Sharon asked her to stay behind. "Teri, I think your presence here has really made a difference with the women."

"How so?" Teri asked.

"Did you notice how some women were silent last time you came?"

"Yes, and I was too."

"And did you notice how each one spoke this week? There was not one silent person in the room."

"Yes I did, and I really enjoyed sharing one to another."

"Well, what you experienced during the last session is what generally happens on a regular basis. But this time was very different. Once you spoke up, the others seemed to be much more comfortable speaking up and sharing."

"Oh, that's wonderful, but I don't think I can take the credit for that. It really had nothing to do with me."

"I beg to differ. I believe the women see you and believe if you can do it, they can do it."

"Yeah, but what would make them feel that way?"

"It just may have something to do with you being a medical doctor. They may not know your personal reputation, but doctors carry a lot of prestige and do not normally share their lives in open forums. Listening to you open up somehow gave them the strength to do so as well."

"That's powerful. But, Sharon, just in case you didn't realize it, you are a doctor also."

"Yes, but I am the host, so they expect me to talk."

"I'm glad my presence made a difference because I know opening up and talking about the past is a catalyst to healing."

"That is correct. Keeping everything bottled up inside can serve to becoming a cancer that will only fester and do harm."

"Yes, don't I know it," Teri agreed remembering the turmoil that grew when she failed to talk about her past.

35

Two and a half months later

The middle of summer had finally arrived, and it had been two years since Reggie and Teri had gone on vacation. Because they had taken a land trip on the last vacation, Teri thought it would be nice to take a cruise. So, off to the Caribbean they would go.

Teri meticulously packed her daughter's overnight bags as well as her own suitcase for the seven-day cruise. She knew she would miss her baby, but at the same time, she was anxious to get some alone time with her honey. While, Teri was packing, Reggie was cleaning out the truck for the drive to the debarkation point at the Long Beach Pier. Afterward, he grabbed his own neatly folded clothes and placed them into his suitcase. He loaded up the truck, helped his wife and daughter to get safely inside, and off they went.

About thirty minutes later, they pulled up to Parker and Noel's home. Hearing their truck pull up, their niece and nephews ran out to greet them. They were excited that their baby cousin was coming to stay with them for a week. Regina would be driven to Priscilla's house each day along with her cousins. Although

Priscilla's arm was out of the cast, Reggie and Teri did not want to put too much on her while she was going through the process of having her bones strengthened, so they opted to leave her with Parker.

After Teri spent twenty minutes saying goodbye and providing a list of instructions, Reggie was finally able to convince his wife that they needed to go or they would miss the ship. Slowly, she handed her daughter over to Noel, after one last kiss.

"Mommy loves you, Monae," she crooned.

"Daddy, too!" Reggie chimed in, while pulling on the back of his wife's shirt.

Back in the truck, they returned to the freeway and headed to Long Beach. The anticipation of the trip began to set in for both of them. As they boarded the ship, Teri thought about everything they had gone through from the time they returned to LAX from Cancun two years ago.

First, there was the drive-by shooting of Jessica Chavez and the surgery. Next were the announcements of Teri's pregnancy and Reggie's assignment to design *NASA*'s space shuttle *Forager*.

Then, there was the issuance of the subpoena and the impending trial. Following the start of the trial was Teri's trip to the emergency room and her week of bed rest. Once she returned back to the trial a week later and the defense presented its case, the verdict came down of innocent! Then, there was the engineers' success of the building of *Forager* although there were a few hiccups along the way. Afterward, the news of Jessica walking came. Then, of course, there was the drama with Parker and Noel, which finally worked itself out. Next came the most exciting news of all: the birth of Reggie and Teri's daughter Regina Monae.

Then to add in another sour note was Priscilla's diagnosis of osteoporosis, but they were praying for the best. Then, Teri and

Reggie experienced icing on their cake; Teri had begun therapy, and now, she was on the winning end. It had certainly been a busy two years.

Aboard the ship, after having settled into their cabin, Reggie and Teri decided to hit the lunch buffet that was already spread for the passengers. They figured they would begin to enjoy themselves right away even though they had not yet left the port. While Reggie heaped his plate high with baked salmon, cheese enchiladas and slice prime rib, Teri opted for raw salmon, capers, sliced tomatoes, cream cheese, and a bagel. They had iced tea to drink and plenty of desserts to choose from. Teri was still working off her baby fat and decided she would not begin on the desserts on day one. She knew if she did, it would be a hard pattern to break.

After lunch, Reggie and Teri stood holding hands by the railing of the ship and watched the ship leave shore. Teri felt all the negativity that she had ever experienced in her life was being left behind and that she was soaring into a brighter future. She truly thanked God for the life He had blessed her with, but she thanked Him even more for the cleaning up process, the renewal process, and the process of refreshing. She knew everything she was experiencing now would help her to be a better mother to her daughter and a better wife to her husband.

Feeling his wife's sense of calm, Reggie placed his arm around her waist and drew her close to him. Looking into her eyes, he said, "You are so beautiful, and I am thankful to spend the next seven days alone with you."

"Thank you, honey. I am looking forward to it as well."

"Great, so let the games begin." Teri knew what that meant.

They went back to their cabin, changed their clothes, put on their bathing suits, and grabbed their beach ball. Reggie and Teri loved playing volleyball in the pool. And inevitably, others soon joined in the fun. Reggie and Teri did not mind one bit. They quickly formed teams: men against the women. It was on- let the Battle of the Sexes go forth!

After a good forty-five minutes of playing, the men beat the women with a score of 6-3. To celebrate their victory, the men treated the women to an island drink. The women graciously received their drinks, lifted up their glasses and toasted the men for being so thoughtful in their win and not rubbing their faces in their defeat.

The rest of the vacation went exactly the same way. There was much laughter and much fun that the couple experienced whether alone or with new people they had met aboard the ship.

In the midst of the fun, Teri and Reggie could not help but to miss their baby girl. They thought of her often, but they knew she had been left in good hands.

Throughout the seven days, Reggie and Teri had several opportunities for heart-to-heart conversations. These conversations helped them to draw closer and closer together. They themselves could not even imagine that there was room for them to draw closer because they were already so very close. But it happened, and they relished in it.

When time drew near for the vacation to come a close, the couple felt a little sad that their alone time was coming to an end. They vowed that they would not wait until their annual vacation to spend time alone. They decided taking mini vacations at least once a quarter would definitely work out better for them and their relationship.

36

A couple of weeks after Reggie and Teri returned from the Caribbean cruise, Teri was ready to continue her counseling sessions. After her first three sessions, she learned Sharon's warning about changes in temperament had been valid. Sharon, however, did not leave the women without tools to combat the changes. She gave them a handbook of methods they could use to effectively deal with them. Teri found the methods particularly helpful.

One day after work, Teri went by her mother's home to pick up her daughter. Prior to Teri's arrival, one of Priscilla's male friends, who was sweet on her had stopped by. When Teri walked in, she saw the man leaning over Regina's swing cooing at her, and Priscilla was nowhere around. Seeing him, Teri launched into protective-mother mode, as she automatically thought something perverse was going on.

"Hey, what are you doing?" Teri yelled out. Teri's outburst startled the man, and he immediately turned around to see who had a problem with him.

Seeing Teri, he responded, "I was just saying hello to the beautiful baby."

"I would thank you to keep your distance from my daughter," Teri retorted as she walked past the man and lifted Regina from her swing. At that moment, Priscilla entered the room.

"What is all the commotion in here?" Priscilla asked in utter surprise at the level of her daughter's voice. She had never known Teri to disrespect any of her friends and couldn't understand what would make her do it now.

"Your guest was hovering over Monae," Teri said accusingly while looking straight at the man and holding her daughter ever so close.

"Hovering, you say?" the man responded.

"Is there something about that word you don't understand?" Teri asked.

"Okay, look you two. Would someone please tell me what is going on?" Priscilla interjected.

"When I walked in, I saw this man hovering over Monae's swing."

"I was simply admiring the beautiful baby and the unique sweater she is wearing. I have not seen a stitch pattern like that since my wife passed some years ago."

"Stitch pattern?" Teri questioned in a much calmer tone.

"He is referring to the stitch pattern in the baby's sweater."

"Mom, please don't tell me you are buying into this."

"There is nothing to buy into, sweetheart. He had just mentioned the stitches before I went to get the iced tea," she said as she lifted the pitcher of tea.

"Oh, I see," Teri said looking rather embarrassed.

"I think you owe Mr. Winters an apology."

"No, she doesn't," Mr. Winters interjected. "A mother should be concerned about who is around her children. She was only being concerned."

"Actually, my mother is right. I do owe you an apology. Being concerned about my daughter's safety, I jumped to conclusions. I apologize for that, Mr. Winters."

"I understand, dear heart, and I accept your apology. Why don't we all have a seat and enjoy some of the iced tea your mother made?" Both Priscilla and Teri consented to enjoying a tall glass of iced tea. It was a cool, needed refreshment in the midst of the summer heat.

As Teri drove home, she had mixed feelings. On one hand, she felt horrible for disrespecting an elderly man and for jumping to conclusions about his intentions. But, on the other hand, she felt good that she dealt with the 'supposed' issue openly and confronted the 'would be' perpetrator. In her past experiences, she had never confronted any of her abusers. She always kept silent. From her group sessions, she learned keeping silent did more harm than good.

Overall, Teri was proud of herself, but she knew she had a long way to go. Being suspicious about everyone who came in contact with her daughter would not work out too well. She knew she had to gain more trust of the world at large, without being naively trusting. She vowed to gain a healthy balance of trust. She loved herself enough to want something better, and she loved the gift God had given her enough to provide a stable environment for her. She would do so by continuing to receive counseling, both in group sessions and in one-on-one sessions.

Six months later, Teri had been attending therapy sessions regularly and had seen a remarkable change in herself and in her overall countenance. She was truly in recovery, and it was all due to admitting she had a problem and wanting to get some help to deal with the problem head on.

Gift of Salvation
for
Non-Believers

"For all have sinned, and come short of the glory of God."
Romans 3:23

This section was written especially for non-believers, those who have not accepted the gift of salvation. The gift of salvation saves souls from eternal damnation and is a free gift offered by God himself. John 3:16-18 says, *"For God so loved the world, that he gave his only begotten Son, that whosoever believeth in him should not perish, but have everlasting life. For God sent not his Son into the world to condemn the world; but that the world through him might be saved. He that believeth on him is not condemned: but he that believeth not is condemned already, because he hath not believed in the name of the only begotten Son of God."* This section of scripture tells us God's purpose for giving His son Jesus to the world. The world was in a bad condition. The world was overwrought with sin; the people were living for fleshly desires rather than for God's desires.

As a result of the world's conditions, God decided that He would offer the perfect sacrifice that would save the world from being a place where people were lost and had no hope. He decided that His own son could stand in proxy for the sin-filled world, taking all sin upon Himself.

So Jesus came, born of a virgin, to save this dying world. He walked on this Earth for 33 ½ years, doing the work of His Heavenly Father. At the appointed time, He died by way of crucifixion upon a cross at Calvary, on Golgatha's hill. He shed his blood and died for you and for me. Because His blood was pure, it paid the penalty for all unrighteousness and gave those who believe in Him direct access to His father's throne.

Scripture tells us in Matthew 27:51 that the veil of the temple was ripped in two from top to bottom, at the moment that Jesus' spirit left His body. As a result of the veil's removal, we are no longer required to have a high priest make intercession for us. We, as the children of the Most High God, are able to approach the throne God for ourselves, and Jesus sits on the right hand of the Father making intercession for us.

But what is even more miraculous than God offering His own son as the perfect sacrifice was the fact that when Jesus was placed in grave clothes and placed in a tomb, He only remained there until the third day. God would not have it that His son would remain in the heart of the Earth forever. In order for people to believe in the awesome power of God and His dear son Jesus, a miracle had to be performed. So, on the third day, after Jesus died on the cross, He was resurrected, demonstrating the omnipotence of God. This very act was the act that would cause people to believe in a god that reigns supreme and holds the power of the universe in His very hands, a god that could save them from themselves.

Today, if you are an unbeliever, you can change your destiny. You can change where you will spend your eternity.

Our Heavenly Father gives us the freedom of choice about how we want to live our life here on Earth and how we want to spend eternity. In Deuteronomy 30:19, God boldly declares, "*I call heaven and earth to record this day against you, that I have set before you life and death, blessing and cursing: therefore choose life, that both thou and thy seed may live.*"

So, dear friend what choice will you make today? Will you spend your eternity with the Creator or will you suffer Hell's eternal flames? Again, the choice is yours. Just as the men aboard the ship who were with Jonah became believers, you too can make a choice to accept the only one and true living God as your god.

If after reading the above passages, you have decided that you want to spend your eternity in Heaven with God, the creator, and His son Jesus, and the Holy Spirit, read through what has affectionately come to be known as the Roman's Road. This is the road to salvation. As you read through the scriptures that comprise the Roman's Road, you will also read the explanation for each scripture so you will have clarity about what you are reading and confessing.

The Roman's Road to Salvation

The road to salvation begins with Romans 3:23 which declares, "*For all have sinned, and come short of the glory of God.*" This scripture explains that everyone has come short of God's glory and needs redemption. Then Romans 6:23a states, "*For the wages of sin is death.*" Here, we learn that the consequence of living a life of sin is death. Everyone will experience physical death as a result of the sin committed in the garden of Eden, but those who commit themselves to a life of sin will suffer eternal damnation in the lake of fire (Rev. 19).

Continue with the rest of verse 6:23 that says, "*but the gift of God is eternal life through Jesus Christ our Lord.*" There is an alternative to suffering eternal damnation. We can accept the gift of salvation by accepting Jesus as our personal lord and savior. Then, Romans 5:8 says, "*But God commendeth his love toward us, in that, while we were yet sinners, Christ died for us.*" We are able to receive the gift of salvation because Christ came to Earth and shed His blood for us on the cross.

Continue to Romans 10: 9-10 which says, "*That if thou shalt confess with thy mouth the Lord Jesus, and shalt believe in thine heart that God hath raised him from the dead, thou shalt be saved. For with the heart man believeth unto righteousness; and with the mouth confession is made unto salvation.*" If we confess with our mouths that Jesus is the son of God, that he came and died for our sins, and that God raised Him from the dead, we will receive salvation.

Finish with Romans 10:13, which states, "*For whosoever shall call upon the name of the Lord shall be saved.*" Call upon the name of God by saying these words, "**Lord Jesus, come into my heart and save me Lord. I believe that you are the Son of God who came and died on the cross for my sins. I believe that you rose from the grave. I also believe that you now sit in heaven on the right side of the Father, making intersession for me. I accept you as my Lord and my Savior.**"

Now that you have confessed with your mouth that Jesus is the son of God and that He died for our sins and rose from the grave, **YOU ARE NOW SAVED!!!!** You will spend your eternity in heaven.

The next step is very important- you must find a bible-based church that teaches the word of God and confesses the Lord Jesus Christ to be the son of God. Don't delay. Do this immediately. Do not leave yourself open to the enemy. Get connected with the saints of the Most High God and keep yourself covered with the unspotted blood of the lamb.

Here is my prayer for you.

Father God,

I thank you for the opportunity to minister your word to the unsaved, the unchurched, and the uncommitted. Father God, I pray now for the souls who have just received the gift of salvation. Lord Father, they have opened their hearts to you, and I know that you have received them into your kingdom and written their names in the Book of Life. Father God, I pray that you will touch their lives and show yourself mightily before them. Let their eyes be opened by the scales falling off, allowing them to see clearly.

Father God, I even pray for the backslider, those who have turned away from you after receiving the gift of salvation. You said in your word that you desire that none would perish. So Lord, I send your word to them right now praying that they would confess the iniquity in their heart, repent, and turn from their evil ways, so that they may receive a life of abundance. You said in your word in Matthew Chapter 14, that every knee shall bow before you and every tongue will confess that Jesus is Lord.

Father God, I pray now that we all come under subjection to your word and that we will humbly submit our lives to you. I ask all these things in the name of my Lord and Savior Jesus Christ.

Amen, Amen, Amen!!!!

I will continue to pray for your success in your walk with God. Remember, this spiritual walk that you are about to embark on will not be an easy walk, but remember, the race is not given to the swift but to those who endure to the end.

Be blessed with heaven's best. I love you!

ABOUT THE AUTHOR

Dr. Cassundra White-Elliott resides in California with her family, where as an English/Education professor she works for various community colleges and universities.

When writing, she writes with the direction of the Holy Spirit, in an effort to share with God's people all that He has for them.

In addition to teaching and writing, Dr. White-Elliott also serves as an evangelistic teacher. She is also the founder of International Women's Commission, a ministry that serves the needs of the entire person, by attending to healing the mind, body, soul, and spirit.

Dr. White-Elliott has earned a Ph.D. in Education, a Master's in English Composition, and a Bachelor's in Education.

Dr. White-Elliott is also the founder of CLF Publishing, LLC. For your publishing needs, go online to www.clfpublishing.org.

OTHER BOOKS BY THE AUTHOR

(All books can be purchased at www.creativemindsbookstore)

From Despair, through Determination, to Victory!

A lot can happen during a span of 40 years. The life of Dr. Cassundra White-Elliott has been anything but uneventful. From a fun-loving childhood sprinkled with incidents of abuse to a tumultuous young adulthood to a stable, secure adult life, she has experienced a full life, with much more to come. Her story is inspiring and motivating.

If anyone lacks hope, reading Dr. White-Elliott's autobiography will propel him/her into an attitude of "Maybe I can." This attitude, if nurtured and developed, will grow into an attitude of "Yes, I can." Throughout her life, Cassundra has always held in her heart the belief that she could achieve anything that she had a made-up mind to embark upon. She was determined to achieve her heart's desires, doing what God has called her to do. She takes no credit for herself. All the glory goes to God, for He is her driving force. In Him, she lives, moves, and has her being.

Through the Storm

Through the Storm was duly inspired by the avaricious cloud of depression that decided to hover overhead of my daily existence in the latter part of 2007. Although I found it extremely difficult, I was once again compelled to not be defeated by just another snare that the enemy, the trickster, set for me. Once again, or more appropriately I should say *continuously*, he has exerted pernicious efforts to snatch the very life out of me by causing me to wallow in despair and to believe that I had been overcome by failure when in actuality and all reality, I was just experiencing a temporary setback. During those cloudy days, I had to remind myself daily that even though I was a target of the enemy, I am and will always be a child of the Most High god, Jehovah, who is my rock, my stability.

Unleashed Anger, Anger Unleashed

Preview

Introduction
What Is This Book All About?

As I prepared to embark upon the adventure of writing this book, I had to prepare myself to also be transparent. I have found that being transparent is required in order for healing to transpire, healing for all those that peruse the pages of this book and myself. And I may as well tell you that today, at the onset of this project, I have not been totally delivered from my condition of being an anger-filled person. However, I am definitely a work in progress. I have made strides with the assistance of my Lord and Savior, Jesus Christ, who is the head of my life. Without his love, guidance, and teachings, I would not be the woman of God I am today. I shudder to think where I could be instead and will therefore not entertain the thought.

Public Speaking in the Spiritual Arena

Preview

Chapter Two
How Communication Works

Purpose: This chapter will explain the six primary components of communication, identifying their purpose and how they work together.

The Source

In oral communication, the source of information is the speaker. In a church setting, the foundation of the message is God's word, but it is a speaker's interpretation of God's word that is delivered to the audience. As speakers vary, the information may vary but should have a similar essence because the foundational text is the same.

The Message

The message is the collective set of ideas that the speaker (the source) wants to deliver and/or illustrate to the audience. The message can be informative where the speaker informs the audience about a specific set of information. Or, the message may be persuasive in nature if the speaker wants to persuade the audience about conducting themselves in a specific manner, accepting God's commandments, or any number of things.

Where is Your Joppa?

Introduction

Where is Your Joppa? was written for the express purpose of illustrating God's call for obedience in the lives of believers with respect to the individual call that He has on each of our lives. As you read throughout the various chapters, notice that the emphasis is placed on our persistent disobedience in answering God's call in a specific area of our lives. We have become a people who are similar to the Israelites when they found themselves in the middle of the wilderness, following their exodus from Egypt. Before God, they murmured and complained about their current life conditions and failed to be obedient to God's statutes delivered through His servant Moses. Their persistent disobedience caused them to lose the opportunity to see and enter the Promised Land. I ask you, "What has your disobedience cost you?" "Was your disobedience worth what it cost you?" "Do you think about the souls you could have ushered into the kingdom of God?" These are some of the questions that I pray will be answered through your reading of the book.

Mayhem in the Hamptons

Romero and Yolanda optimistically plan for the day that is going to change their lives from being single persons to a couple who is united in holy matrimony. They, along with their parents, close friends and family, fly over to the infamous Hamptons, where only the rich and famous vacation, to have their dream wedding at the five-star Hampton Suites located on a peninsula in the Hamptons. Little do they know that their perfect day will turn out to be less than perfect when their wedding planner Mariesha Coleman suddenly goes missing!

A time when the newlyweds' lives should be filled with joy and the creation of wonderful memories, they are stricken with grief as they desperately try to find clues to help solve Mariesha's disappearance.

Mayhem in the Hamptons is a tale that shares how the horrors of a woman's past can come back to haunt her in more than one way and the impact it can have on anyone who gets in the way.

Preacher's Daughter

Tinisha, the daughter of a preacher, is a twenty-six year old God-fearing young woman endeavoring to complete law school so that she can make her mark in the courtroom. Working in one of the late-night clubs in Hollywood to earn money to pay her own way through school, Tinisha soon learns that life doesn't always go as planned. Finding her strength in her faith, Tinisha constantly finds herself praying as she watches God move miraculously in her life.

Preacher's Son

Romero Turner is a private investigator with a promising future. As he continues to build his career, he is excited about the cases he undertakes. However, his father Pastor Theodore Turner has other plans for his son's life. In the midst of trying to save his client's husband from Sylvester Domingo, a ruthless crime lord, Romero must try to salvage his relationship with his father. He must decide if ministry or life as a detective is in his future.

Lord, Teach Me to be a Blessing!

Lord, Teach Me to be a Blessing! will change a person's mentality from being centered around "me, myself, and I" to focusing on "others."

The world system teaches us that it is acceptable to place ourselves above others in an attempt to get ahead and even to survive. Herbert Spencer coined the phrase *'survival of the fittest'* after reading Charles Darwin's theory of evolution. This concept of surpassing and outdoing others is the world's philosophy.

However, the word of God does not subscribe to or promote this self-centered ideology, and therefore, neither should believers. We must hold fast to the truths outlined in Holy Scripture: *"Love thy neighbor as you love thyself"* (James 2:8) and *"It is more blessed to give than to receive"* (Acts 20:35). While holding God's truths to be self-evident, we must demonstrate them to others, thereby showing them the way of the Lord of how to be a blessing to someone *rather* than looking to receive a blessing.

This is the very purpose of this book: to change the mentality of the world from being *self*-centered to *other* centered.

After the Dust Settles

Throughout the journey of life, we all experience ups and downs and joys and pains. Most of us successfully find solutions to the situations/problems we encounter, but we often avoid dealing with the attached emotions. If we continue to ignore the emotions of pain, hurt, disappointment, anger, etc., we set ourselves up for destruction. Our families, our cultures, and our society tell us to be strong, to keep our chin up, and to grin and bear it. However, these methods of avoidance can lead us to strokes due to the undue amount of pressure we place on ourselves and/or mental illness from being unable to cope with the emotional baggage we have accumulated.

In *After the Dust Settles,* Dr. C. White-Elliott shares several situations that we all may encounter at one time or another in our lifetime and how to successfully navigate through them, so we can find ourselves emotionally healthy after the dust has settled and the situation has been rectified.

Begin reading today and experience a better tomorrow!

A Diamond in the Rough

A Diamond in the Rough Architecture Firm was built and is owned and operated by lead architect Kyra Fraser. For the last five years, Kyra has been extremely successful in business, but her love life leaves much to be desired.

Kyra has set high standards for herself and does not wish to take a man in any condition and attempt to make him over. She is looking for someone who is drama free, well educated, very cultured, fun-loving, good looking, self-motivated, and the list goes on.

Will Kyra find the man of her dreams, or will her dream just continue to be a dream?

As you delve into this page-turning novel, Kyra's reality will unfold as you are drawn into her world of design, love and office drama-which includes her best friend's husband who is looking for love in all the wrong places.

365 Days of Encouragement

Just as our brain requires oxygen obtained from the air we breathe to sustain our mortal bodies, our spirit requires revitalization and encouragement in order to be strengthened each and every day of our lives. The revitalization and encouragement needed for the spirit of man comes directly from the word of God and assists us in walking according to the way of our heavenly Father. 365 Days of Encouragement provides a scripture a day for each day of the year. Along with the daily scripture is a brief note of commentary also for the benefit of edifying the saints of God.

It is my prayer that the people of God would live a fulfilled life through Christ Jesus. Knowing His word and understanding we can walk in the fulfillment thereof is empowering. We are instructed in II Timothy 2:15, "Study to shew thyself approved unto God, a workman that needeth not to be ashamed, rightly dividing the word of truth" (KJV). Take an opportunity to delve further into the word of God, to know His statutes and to allow your own personal life to be edified, so you can be equipped to bring glory to God and lived a fulfilled life.

A Mother's Heart

A Mother's Heart shares the unconditional love of mothers through a compilation of testimonies. Each testimony serves as a tribute to a special mother. The children of the represented mothers have lovingly written about their childhood, young adult life and/or older adult experiences they shared with their mother. As you read the writers' reflections, you will feel the expressions of love exude from the pages.

The purpose of this book is two-fold. First, it honors those mothers who stood by their children through the trials of life and showered them with unconditional love. Second, the book is a source of encouragement for mothers who may feel inadequate and question whether or not they are actually suited for motherhood. Our advice to mothers is, "Be encouraged; the journey of motherhood may seem daunting at times and you may shed some tears, but your children will never forget the love you have shown them and instilled in them to share with others."

Mothers may not be perfect, but they are definitely unmatched by any other category of person on God's green Earth!